BACON AND BEANS FROM A GOLD PAN

Bacon and Beans from a Gold Pan

GEORGE HOEPER

AS TOLD BY

JESSE L. COFFEY

Publishers of Fine Books

Fresno, California 1988

LIBRARY OF CONGRESS CATALOG CARD NUMBER 76-171284
ISBN 0-944194-12-5
ISBN 0-944194-13-3 PAPER

CONTENTS

INTRODUCTION

There are still quite a few, in California and the Far West, who can remember the crushing overnight poverty that came with the stock market crash and the bank closings of the early 1930s.

And, there is another handful who can recall what action those affected took to recover from the vast financial entanglements of that era. They recall that some folks sat back and waited for a job to appear or for "relief" from the federal government. Others, more fiercely independent, returned to the occupation that had brought their grandparents to California in the first place, the occupation of mining gold from the streams and crevices of the gold-rich region of central California known as the Mother Lode.

As a youngster, George Hoeper was, in retrospect, a keen observer of the times. He knew from whence the "bacon and beans" money of those Great Depression days came, for he saw the raw gold exchanged for the necessary commodities of life. Later on, George worked in a gold mine near Auburn, so he knows the times of which he reports.

Thus, is told the authentic story of Dot and Jesse Coffey. It is the warm, credible, human interest story of a man and his wife and how they made their way in a labyrinth of financial recovery from 1932 to the beginnings of World War II. Their adventures take them from the rich placers of Agua Fria Creek in Mariposa County to the well-worn placer mines of the Yuba River near Downieville, Sierra County. All of the Mother Lode lies in between.

To the author's lasting glory, he has included a lost mine story, some adventures in the Sierra Butte area of Sierra County (the purported site of the fabulous Gold Lake) and the day-to-day hankerings of a generation of people like the Coffeys, who were too proud to call it quits.

Clearly, George Hoeper has struck gold with a manuscript that brings to life a generation of prudence that brought prosperity of a sort to central California during one of the nation's darkest hours. This book is a tribute to that generation and a microcosm of a life-style now nearly forgotten.

DONALD I. SEGERSTROM
PRESIDENT, AMERICAN GOLD MINING ASSOC.
SONORA, CALIFORNIA

MAY 21, 1971

GOLD FEVER

Though bacon and beans,
With dandlion greens,
  May dismay us,
A Mother Lode stream
With one golden seam
  Could repay us.

While in God we trust
That our burning lust
  Not betray us,
As our shovels thrust
For nuggets and dust
  In San Andreas.

C. M. Vandeburg
June 1, 1971

BACON AND BEANS FROM A GOLD PAN

CHAPTER I

THE VENTURE

It was early October, and there was a chill in the afternoon air as Dot and I, our meager belongings stacked around us, stood viewing that little clearing on the banks of Agua Fria Creek surveying what was to be our new home.

This was gold country—this was the Mother Lode.

This lonely little canyon which wound its way through the oak- and Digger pine-covered foothills of California's Mariposa County had been one of the spots where, in gold rush days, the 49ers had "struck it rich." First had come the Americans and Mexicans in 1849 and '50, and after them the Chinese, to pick over what the ever-hurrying white men had missed.

And now, in this Depression year, Dot and I, newly married, had come here on the premise that the "old-timers" and the Chinese who followed them had not found it all. With pan and sluice box we would mine this creek and I, at least, believed there was still enough gold here to feed and clothe us, to provide a living. It would be better, we told ourselves, than standing in a bread line, than living jobless in a city, each day going further into debt.

We had married in San Jose. Between us we had eighteen dollars, a tiny apartment with paint-peeled walls in a huge, rambling old building shared by cockroaches and neighbors with innumerable, small, grimy-faced children who spent most of their waking hours squalling or fighting.

Only change the new year brought with it was closure of the cannery where I had been employed for twelve years as a field manager, and with its closure came the loss of my job. The remainder of that winter and spring was one of utter frustration.

There were virtually no jobs, but finally, through WPA, I managed to obtain a couple of months work at San Jose State College. This, at least, gave us eating money and helped pay back bills.

But the job at the college ended. Once again I found myself plodding miles each day from employment agency to agency, standing in lines of jobless men at mills and factories, and always with the same result. We still had my old Chevvy, but shoe leather was cheaper than gas. I seldom drove it.

But we managed to hold on, bolstered by the few dollars saved from my job at the college, and then, in late spring, came a break.

My old boss phoned me from the cannery.

"It's only a seasonal job, but it will keep you going until September. It's the best I can offer you, Jess," he said.

I went to work next day, contracting for fruit and vegetable crops and, later in the summer, supervising their picking, packing, and shipment. But, as I worked, I kept thinking of the Sierra foothills where, as a boy, I had learned to pan and sluice for gold, and an idea began forming in my mind.

Even before we married I had often told Dot how, as a boy, I had mined the rivers and creeks—sniping, the old-timers called it. A couple of times we had made trips to the mountains where Dot learned to use a gold pan and how a sluice box works. Each time we had found gold.

August arrived, and before I knew it we were into the first weeks of September, and then came notice from the cannery that in exactly two weeks it was shutting down.

That night, in our drab little apartment, I explained my idea to Dot.

There was a place in Mariposa County, I explained, where I was pretty sure that with sluice box and gold pan we could make at least a couple of dollars a day. It was part of the old John C. Frémont ranch which had been granted to him by the Spanish. It was called Agua Fria Creek.

"Nobody will bother us there—we can build a tenthouse and get some camping equipment—and it will be a helluva lot better than this hand-to-mouth existence we're leading here in the city."

Even before I got through my little prepared speech, Dot was convinced.

The next two weeks were ones of hectic preparation. My job was ending and I was working long hours trying to tie up all the loose ends. At the same time, there was a tent to buy, camping equipment to beg and borrow, food to purchase, and long lists of minor items to be sure we didn't forget.

When you are up in the mountains the corner drugstore and the grocery store are a long ways away, and you either remember the things you need before you start, or you do without.

From one couple we borrowed a camp bed, from other friends a small, sheet-iron tent stove. We found a good ten-by-twelve tent at a secondhand store, and I found a little two-wheel trailer for five dollars that we could tow behind the Chevvy.

Ranchers who heard of my plans pressed gifts of dried fruit on us and many other items that would be useful.

One of my last purchases was a little, single barreled .410 shotgun, for the country we were going into teemed with Cottontail rabbits, gray squirrel, and quail. Anyone in the mountains in those days under circumstances like ours lived off the country as much as he could.

My job came to a close, and it was with few regrets we handed the key of our apartment over to the landlord three days later, packed the last of our gear on the trailer, and headed for Mariposa County and the mountains.

The fall sunshine was golden as we rolled through the lower San Joaquin Valley and stopped at Ceres to visit my dad and to tell him we were going, and of our plans.

I don't think I've ever seen Dot any happier or enthused about anything in all our married life. And her enthusiasm was contagious. Ladybug, our little fox terrier, barked at passing cars and stuck her head far out of the car window to catch the wind. Dot had to keep continually pulling her back in.

We sang as we drove, and when we arrived at Dad's place he, too, became enthusiastic, and immediately announced he was going with us to help us get settled in our camp.

We stayed overnight in Ceres and dawn was barely breaking when I started the old Chevvy and Dad cranked up his Model T pickup.

Now, at one o'clock this October afternoon we stood looking at Agua Fria Creek, a small, shallow river winding clear and glistening between the dark colored rocks that lined its rugged shoreline.

"There's gold here," I told Dot, "all we gotta do is find it."

But there was more to do than simply go gold hunting. We had a camp to build. Dad and I, leaving Dot and Ladybug looking small and lonely among our scattered duffle, took off for Mariposa six miles away, to buy the lumber that would build our tenthouse.

The town of Mariposa straddled narrow, twisting Highway 49, a cluster of weatherbeaten frame houses in various stages of disrepair, basking in the warm, foothill sun.

The old, wooden county courthouse, that had already seen its first decade when President Lincoln was assassinated, stood off Main Street at one side of the little business district.

Several of the other buildings were of native stone and mortar construction, built in the early gold rush days when the town's population numbered in the thousands. The old hotel where travelers sometimes still stopped and the general store were now the focal points of activity. As we drove slowly down the dusty, chuckholed street, we fell under the careful scrutiny of the town loungers who held down the benches in front of each. "The spit and whittle club," the townspeople called them, and there were few subjects or events that did not get full discussion and considerable elaboration before they were completely hashed out by those old bench warmers.

At that time Mariposa probably had about six hundred people living in and around it. Most of these residents were either involved or had been involved at one time or another in some kind of mining.

The lumber yard was on the edge of town and the proprietor, a big, bushy-haired, husky man, immediately sized us up and surmised what we were going to do with the lumber.

"Snipers. Gonna go down and mine on the Agua Fria, I'll bet." It was more of a statement than a question. In fact, he did not even wait for an answer.

"Well, I'll tell you boys somethin'—she's damn slim pickin's down there—damn well worked out. The old-timers cleaned her up pretty good and the Chinamen took what they left. That country's been mined and prospected for pretty near a hundred years now, and today I'll bet there's forty snipers camped along that twenty miles of creek—damn few of 'em makin' enough to buy bread and beans."

He paused to wipe the sweat off his face with a big red bandanna, then heaved a few more boards onto the trailer.

"These snipers, they come and go all the time—come here with a couple of dollars and high hopes, and six weeks later they leave dead broke. Half of 'em have to hock their spare tire or something to get gas enough to leave town. Now, don't get me wrong—I ain't tryin' to discourage—just telling you the truth."

The last of the lumber—rough cut pine boards—was piled on our trailer and we headed back through town and to our campsite. But somehow, that lumberyard owner's words kept ringing in my ears. Even though I certainly did not believe all of his prophesies of doom, the sun somehow did not seem to be shining so brightly on the way back to camp. I planned to say nothing of this to my wife.

Dot had a fire going by the time we arrived at the creek with our load, and already she was rustling through the boxes and sacks for the dishes and food for supper.

Smoke from the driftwood fire filled the little clearing with its mellow fragrance, and this, added to the smell of perking coffee, whetted our appetites.

We ate supper as the last rays of the fall sun were hitting the tops of the ridges above us, and then, after washing the dishes, sat around the glowing campfire for a long time, planning the coming day's projects. Finally, the fire died down and the evening chill drove us to bed.

Shortly after daylight I was awakened by a woodpecker hammering on a dead limb and the rattle of pots and pans. Dad already was up and had the morning campfire going.

By sunup we were eating breakfast and minutes later the day's work was underway.

Using flat slabs of slate rock we constructed the foundation for the tenthouse and, on that, when it had reached the height of about a foot, we placed our foundation timbers and floor joists.

The floor and four-foot walls of the tenthouse were of rough pine boards, and above them went the rafter framework on which the tent itself would set.

With the height of the board walls, plus the three-foot canvas walls of the tent, we had six-foot walls inside our tenthouse.

We added a small, floorless front porch, installed the stove, and then took up the task of building shelves, a table, and benches.

While Dot began moving our supplies indoors, Dad and I took up the next task, that of digging a hole some fifty yards from the tenthouse and constructing a canvas-covered one-holer that was immediately dubbed the Rose Room.

There was a garbage pit to dig, and a small spring from which issued a flow of cold, clear water had to be enlarged and brush cleared away from it. It was one of those days when time seemed to fly and there still were a dozen different chores to be done when Dot announced that supper was ready.

Baked beans never had tasted so good before and this night there was no sitting up late around a campfire. We were all dead tired from a full day of exertion.

I was anxious to get to mining, but there still were a number of pretty important things to be done.

Winter was not so far away as we would have liked to believe, and a supply of wood is a pretty necessary thing when it is all you have to depend on for both cooking and heat.

And, paradoxically, the weather still was dry and there was still some danger of wildfire. So, as a safety measure against fire, I cleared all of the stray brush out of the area for fifty yards around our camp and scraped a bare fire protection line around the tenthouse.

Those were the days before chain saws and my woodcutting tools were simply an ax and a bucksaw. There is more truth than poetry in the old saying about cutting your own wood and getting warm twice. Dry oak and manzanita were plentiful, and all that it required to build up a good woodpile was plenty of energy.

By midafternoon I had a respectable pile of wood, enough to last us a week or more, at least. With a couple of our remaining pine boards and some Digger pine bark, I made a crude little shelter to protect the wood from the rain, and the last of our major camp-making chores was done.

It was with considerable satisfaction the three of us surveyed our accomplishments of the past couple of days. As we stood there taking our short breathing spell, Dad announced it was about time he was heading back for Ceres.

The old Model T started with its usual clattering roar, and with a wave of goodbye and the announcement that he would be back in a couple of weeks to see how we were making it, my dad was on his way.

Only the short end of the afternoon remained, but the urge to explore the gold mining possibilities of the little creek was too great to resist.

Ever since we had arrived I had been eying a small riffle a hundred yards upstream from camp where an expanse of rough bedrock, partially covered by a thin layer of creek gravel, lay exposed. It was a likely looking spot.

With gold pan and shovel I made my way up to the rapids and, at the water's edge, chose a gravel filled crevice several inches wide which appeared to provide a natural trap for gold.

Carefully, I filled the pan, digging deep into the bottom of the crevice, and then, breathing a silent prayer, stepped to the creek and began working the pan of gravel with a swirling motion.

The water was so cold it stung my hands, but slowly, carefully, I washed away the excess gravel.

Gold, even though it be in the finest of flakes, has a high specific gravity which forces it to the bottom of the pan.

There was only a half-handful of fine gravel and black sand remaining in the pan when suddenly, as I slowly swept the water through it, I saw the first bright gleam of yellow metal.

They were only specks, the largest perhaps half the size of a match head, but there was no mistaking that yellow glitter—it was gold.

Behind me I heard a suppressed gasp. I turned and there was Dot, looking over my shoulder. Her eyes were filled with excitement.

I don't suppose there was ten cents in the whole pan, but from Dot's reaction you would have thought the bottom of the pan was lined with nuggets.

I tried a second pan, and a third, and each time I came up

with fine gold. A fourth panful produced a tiny nugget not quite so large as a cantaloupe seed and even I could not suppress a thrill of excitement.

But, by now my hands were numbed and blue from exposure to the cold water, and although it seemed I had been there only a few minutes, a full hour had slipped by.

"That's all for today," I told Dot.

"Tomorrow we'll get a sluice box going and we'll be able to handle this gravel four times as fast as we can with a gold pan. And right now, my hands won't take any more of that water. I sure know now why they call it Agua Fria Creek."

We returned to camp. With evening on its way, I took the little .410 shotgun and, accompanied by Ladybug, began working my way along the edge of a brush-bordered swale that stretched up the canyon from camp. Within a half hour we were back with two cottontails that would provide the meat for tomorrow night's stew.

Dusk had fallen by the time I reached the tenthouse and at the edge of our clearing I paused for a moment to roll a cigarette.

Within the tenthouse I could see the glow of the kerosene lamp, and smoke wafted lazily from the chimney of our little stove where Dot was preparing supper. I took a deep drag, exhaled slowly, and for the first time in many months, a sense of security and quiet satisfaction crept over me.

CHAPTER II

MINING AGUA FRIA CREEK

A SNIPER'S SLUICE BOX IS SIMPLY THREE BOARDS ABOUT SIX FEET IN length nailed together to form a U-shaped trough.

Sides of the box are six or eight inches high, and its flat bottom from ten inches to a foot wide.

In the bottom lies the detachable riffles of wood or heavy wire mesh which catch and hold the particles of gold which work out of the gravel as it washes through the box.

The sluice box sits on legs or is propped up by rocks at an angle which allows the water running through it to carry away the rock and sand shoveled into its upper end. The gold, being heavy, works to the bottom of the sluice box and is caught by the riffles.

One of the requisites of a sniper's sluice box is that it must be light enough to be easily transported, for seldom does a sniper work for long in one place.

A single day's work may clean up a rich spot, and seldom in the days we were mining did we ever find a spot large enough to keep us there for more than a couple of weeks at most.

The advantage of a sluice box is that far more gravel can be worked through one in a day than a man can ever handle with gold pan alone.

If possible, a sniper tries to run water through his sluice box by gravity, but on flat flowing streams and rivers this often is an impossibility. The more affluent among gold miners used a small pump driven by a little gasoline engine, but in the depression days of gold mining these were few and far between.

The other alternative was simply to use a "dip stick," a small bucket on the end of a stick.

This was the method Dot and I employed during our first days of mining—and for many months to come—on Agua Fria Creek.

Our first day, and indeed our first weeks on the Agua Fria, stand out in my mind as though they were only yesterday.

By sunup on our first full day of mining, I had my sluice box set and the first shovelfuls of gravel were washing through it. An hour later Dot arrived and, between the two of us, a constant flow of pay dirt was fed into the box.

I would shovel the surface gravel into the box, and then, as I reached the shallow bedrock, scrape deep into each crevice, cleaning it as thoroughly as if it had been gone over with a vacuum cleaner.

The heaviest gold, and the most gold, always lies deepest in the crevices, and we were after every crumb and grain that rock and gravel held.

Shortly before noon, Dot dug into the cardboard box she had brought with her, took out the coffeepot, and began building a campfire. I paid scant attention to her activities, noticing out of the corner of my eye only that she was building a little fireplace on which to set the old tin percolator.

The fire was blazing merrily, coffee perking, and, some thirty feet away, I was just washing a batch of gravel through the box when there was a sudden "bang." I felt a sharp, stinging blow on the back of my leg, jumped, landed on a wet, slippery rock, and fell down. For an instant I thought I had been shot.

Scrambling to my feet, I saw Dot still was all in one piece but that the fire was scattered and the coffeepot overturned. I still half-believed someone had shot at us, when there was another sharp "pop" and part of our fireplace flew to pieces.

It was only then that I realized what had happened.

My greenhorn wife had gathered pieces of damp slate rock to build her fireplace. Heat of the fire had caused water trapped in tiny seams of the slate rock to condense into steam, and the rock simply exploded.

That was the first of many lessons of the out-of-doors that Dot learned. We ate our noonday sandwiches washed down by creek water instead of hot coffee.

Lunch finished, Dot's curiosity got the better of her and she demanded to see how much gold our morning's work had gained us.

"That gold will all still be right there when we finish the day's work," I told her, but Dot was insistent, and so I carefully lifted the riffles from the box.

Even before I began washing the residual sand from the box into a gold pan, I could see several flecks of gold, and to my surprise, the specks and flakes, and then tiny gold nuggets, multiplied as the water flushed the sand from sluice box into pan.

I had expected to find no coarse gold at all, but as I swirled the gold pan several tiny nuggets about the size of small match heads suddenly made their appearance along with smaller, flatter flakes of alluvial gold, amounting in actual volume to perhaps half a teaspoon.

Dot, leaning over my shoulder watching every move with hushed intensity, let out a yell of excitement as the little nuggets appeared. She slapped me on the back, almost causing the whole gold pan to go flying into the water.

"Oh, Jess, we've hit it—just look at that gold—look at those nuggets! I never thought we'd find anything like this."

It was no great strike and I knew it, but to be sure, it was really better than I had expected. I carefully washed the last of the heavy black sand away from the gold and poured the still wet, shining flakes of yellow metal into the small medicine bottle I carried just for that purpose.

I estimated our morning's work had brought us considerably better than a pennyweight of gold. A pennyweight is worth just about $1.75 at the rate of $35 an ounce.

Carefully replacing the riffles in the sluice box, we resumed shoveling and washing gravel, and spurred by our morning's success both of us worked doubly hard.

At midafternoon I stopped for a short breathing spell to roll a cigarette, only to be informed by my wife there was no time to be wasted in sitting down when there was gold to be mined.

By 3:30 P.M. we had cleared a circle several feet in diameter around the sluice box and in order to keep from having to move the dirt too far, the sluice box would have to be moved.

And, although neither of us realized it until then, we both were pretty well exhausted. Dot suddenly discovered that the shovel handle had worn blisters on both hands.

We called a halt for the day, cleaned the sluice box for the second time, and returned to camp.

As Dot built a fire and began preparing an early supper I dried and weighed our day's find on my gold scales. There was just a trifle less than three pennyweights—a pretty good day's work when I stopped to realize that many men were working ten hours a day on jobs down in the valley for four dollars or less.

Not every day on the Agua Fria was as productive as that first day of mining. At times we worked knee deep in icy water and made only a dollar. Other times we would hit a rich spot and in an hour would take out a half ounce of coarse gold.

The entire length of this little river had been worked, not only by the old-timers, but by other prospectors and snipers. We had to be just a little more careful than the men who had been here before us.

Gold mining the way we did it was a matter of applying knowledge, hard work, and imagination coupled with a bit of luck. We had to find crevices that others had missed, or places where storm waters had washed and swirled, concentrating fine gold in the thin layers of gravel that coated rough bedrock along the stream. We looked for the unlikely places, or spots that others might have passed up because it appeared the work involved would not justify the amount of gold they might produce.

Sometimes we worked close to camp, sometimes a mile or more upstream or downstream from our tenthouse. In summer, with the river at its lowest, we worked the bedrock close to the water's edge, and in winter the rising stream drove us to higher ground where we sought little spots of pay dirt the others might have missed.

It was a rattlesnake that was the cause of our biggest single strike during that year or more that we spent on the Agua Fria.

Dot had stayed in camp that morning and I was walking along the river trail to a little spot we had been sluicing about a mile upstream.

Suddenly, as I rounded a rocky area that lay just below the high waterline of the stream, I was startled by the sharp, unmistakable buzz of a rattlesnake. It lay coiled menacingly at the foot of a large, granite boulder, its ugly, triangular head drawn back to strike, rattles vibrating with that dry, threatening danger.

But, as I moved forward, shovel poised, the big reptile—it was nearly four feet long—slithered swiftly into a shallow cranny beneath the boulder. Determined not to allow the snake to get away, I jabbed and smashed at him with the steel point of the shovel. Finally, after dislodging some of the gravel around the crack under the big rock, I succeeded in dragging the big rattler out and killing it.

It was then I saw the nugget, a solid, smoothly worn piece of gold the size of a large bean.

Hurriedly, I returned to camp for the gold pan, steel crowbar, some blocks of wood, and the car jack from the old Chevvy.

Dot returned with me and within an hour we had pried the big rock from its resting place and, with the aid of the car jack and blocks, rolled it off the tiny spot of gravel it had covered.

From that spot of gravel, six inches deep and little more than two feet square, I panned nine ounces of coarse, raw gold worth $315 at the San Francisco Mint.

The entire operation was completed by noon. We moved other nearby boulders and quarried and cubbyholed under more that were too large to move, but came up with only a trace of colors from these.

I had simply, by utter luck, and with help of an irritable rattlesnake, stumbled onto the one spot in that entire area of the creek that the old-time miners, for some unknown reason, completely missed.

Nor were Dot and I the only ones among the snipers who hit occassional "sweet" spots along the Agua Fria.

One afternoon two snipers, whom we knew only as John and Fred, arrived at our camp, faces beaming with suppressed excitement.

John, a husky man in his fifties, with grizzled beard which he trimmed with scissors and pocket knife, dumped nearly two ounces of pea-sized nuggets and fine gold onto the oilcloth-covered table in our tenthouse.

"Just take a look at that," he exclaimed.

"We got that in just three pans about an hour ago, and the last pan was just as rich as the first! We want to borrow your wheelbarrow, and if you will let us have it, that long sluice box of yours, too. We hit this spot pretty high up on the creekbank and we've got to move the dirt about fifty feet to get it to water where we can set up the sluice box."

The particular spot that John and Fred had found was in a pretty inaccessible location a couple of miles downcanyon and it took them three days to get all of their mining equipment, including my large twelve-foot sluice box and wheelbarrow, to the site.

Most of us along the river didn't work on Sunday. That was a day reserved for trivial camp chores, for just resting and taking it easy. But John and Fred, spurred by the excitement of their find, got their equipment in place late Saturday afternoon and decided to go ahead and spend Sunday mining their new strike.

Late sundown Sunday afternoon, just as Dot and I were finishing dinner, Fred arrived, pushing my wheelbarrow.

"Well, how did it go?" I asked, but even before he answered I knew from his expression that their day had not been any screaming success.

"Oh, it was there, all right—what there was of it," he replied dejectedly.

"It was a strip about four inches wide, four inches deep and about twenty-five feet long, and it was so rich you would hardly believe it—I bet we got seven or eight ounces. But that was every damn bit there was. You couldn't even raise a color on either side of that little strip of gravel."

What Fred and John had done was to find the line of one of the old, original 49er mining claims. In gold rush days the claims on Agua Fria Creek were fifty feet long and ran from high-water mark to high-water mark on each side of the creek. Apparently, the miners who had owned two adjoining claims had each worked up to within inches of his line. Then each, afraid he would infringe on the other's property, had quit, leaving that tiny strip of pay dirt.

It took John and Fred another three days to carry all the equipment back to their camp and return what they had borrowed. Even so, it was a pretty profitable week's work back in those Depression days.

Another sniper—we knew him only as "Red Whiskers"—had his own unique way of mining, and it paid off, but I hardly think the gain was worth the effort. At least, I could never have stood the rigors of his labor.

This was back in the days before anyone had ever heard of scuba diving for gold, but all of us knew there were crevices deep underwater in Agua Fria Creek and other streams and rivers of the Mother Lode that had never been really cleaned out, even by the 49ers.

In some places, it is true, the gold rush miners and Chinese flumed the streams and worked the stream beds right down to bedrock, but in some places fluming was impossible.

Red Whiskers was a huge barrel-chested giant of a man who spokc with a Finnish accent so heavy it was hard to understand him. He was one of the few men who consistently came up with large, heavy nuggets when the rest of us were finding only small pieces and flour gold.

Braving the icy water, Red Whiskers had fashioned himself a sort of homemade snorkel, a piece of rubber hose which he gripped in his mouth while the other end extended to the surface, attached to a float.

With crevicing tools and scrapers Red Whiskers worked below the surface of the water, cleaning the cracks in the bedrock.

Using weights to hold his body down, this great shaggy Finlander would remain submerged for unbelievable lengths of time in that cold water. He usually worked stark naked, winter and summer. When he surfaced, shaking his great shaggy head and red matted beard, blasting air from his oxygen-starved lungs, he looked and sounded like some prehistoric sea monster.

But not all of the snipers who came to the Agua Fria and other streams in hopes of eking out a living by mining gold were rewarded with success.

True, some were lazy, some were simply drunks, but most were people fleeing from the city where there was no employment, who hoped to find enough gold to keep them going until something better came along.

But most were totally inexperienced both in gold mining and in the ways of the out-of-doors. They pitched tents or moved into old abandoned cabins. Some merely had a shelter constructed of a canvas and old boards or strips of rusted sheet iron they had salvaged from some long-abandoned mine.

In those days even a dollar a day would feed and clothe a

man, for he had no rent to pay, no utilities, and the country itself could provide a good part of his living if he knew where to look for it.

A fellow we knew only as Sammy moved onto the river near us and set up a primitive camp a half mile or so upstream.

Admittedly he knew nothing of gold mining, but a friend had told him a man could make a living up in the hills by panning gold. The only problem was, Sammy had never seen a gold pan until he stopped and bought one at the general store in Mariposa on his way to the Agua Fria. His only other mining tool was a shovel.

I spent part of one morning teaching Sammy how to use the gold pan, and later, helped him build a small sluice box. Sammy stayed for a month or so, then moved on, to where or what I cannot say.

A few days after Sammy left, Dot and I were walking past his abandoned camp.

Simply out of curiosity, I walked over to what remained of the board and tarpaper shelter held together by a few rusty nails. In all truth, I had seen better shacks in a hobo jungle.

A few feet behind the tiny dwelling a small pile of still shiny tin cans caught my eye. Idly, I walked over to inspect them. They were all empty dog food cans, yet I knew full well that Sammy, while he had stayed at this camp, had never owned a dog.

As weeks passed, we became acquainted with our more permanent neighbors who lived several miles each way up and down Agua Fria Creek.

And, as time went on, we became sort of a close knit group. We were the permanent residents, so to speak, a cut above the fly-by-nighters who came and went without ever becoming a part of the community. Most of us who were permanent, such as John and Fred, old Red Whiskers, Jack and Bill, and Big Tom had neat, well-built camps or cabins. All of us had proven we were reasonably successful snipers and were proud of it.

The day that Dot and I realized we had become a part of the permanent clan was the afternoon that old Bill walked into camp with a flour sack-wrapped object on his shoulder. It was the latter part of November and deer season had been closed for six weeks.

"Took a little walk with the rifle this morning, and just by accident happened to bump into a big buck. Thought maybe you folks could use some fresh meat since there's more here than I could handle by myself."

From then on that was the way it went. If Dot and I happened to go fishing and caught a few more trout than we could use, we shared them with a neighbor. In summer some of us planted gardens, and there always was an exchange of vegetables.

Fish and game season didn't mean much to the snipers along the rivers in the Sierra country in those days, and the game wardens were well aware of the fact. But the wardens also knew that the men and women in those scattered camps did not hunt or fish for sport or for the fun of killing. Every fish or game animal taken was utilized down to the last scrap.

October now was long gone, November disappeared, and with December came the winter rains—torrential downpours that turned every dry gulch into a live stream and changed the Agua Fria from a meandering creek into a swollen river.

The first storm hit so suddenly and with such vicious fury that it raised the Agua Fria several feet in a single night. Several of the miners, caught unaware, lost sluice boxes and tools they had left where they had been mining on the river's edge. Luckily, Dot and I had been working a piece of higher ground that particular day, and with the exception of a gold pan I had left leaning against a rock beside a pool where I had been panning, we lost nothing.

But it was too wet to try to mine or stay out-of-doors for any length of time, and for the duration of the storm we stayed inside the warm, dry tenthouse, venturing out only to carry in more wood. We listened to the wind-whipped rain spattering against our roof and by light of the little kerosene lamp, read the old magazines and books that had been traded back and forth between camps.

The rain stopped but the river remained high and muddy. Most of the good gravel bars and low bedrock that had paid dividends during the low-water period were now covered and unworkable.

This was the time to turn to the smaller side streams and gullies.

One small creek in particular had interested me for some time, but until now it had been completely dry, lacking even enough water for panning. I had bypassed it in favor of the river, but now this little rill, a tributary of the Agua Fria, was running a fair head of water, and the morning after the rain quit I went exploring.

Up this little steep-sided creek I wandered for more than a mile. My only equipment was shovel, prospecting pick, and a small gold pan. The ground on both sides of the creek showed evidence of early day mining, and here and there were rock walls still standing where early white or Chinese miners had stacked the waste rock from their sluicing.

Now and then I stopped to clean out a likely looking crevice or to sample a belt of gravel that, hopefully, other miners had overlooked, but other than a few fine grains of gold my efforts were fruitless.

At noon I stopped to rest and share a sandwich with Ladybug, who had accompanied me. While smoking a cigarette before resuming my travels, I noticed where the recent high water had eaten into the edge of what appeared to be an ancient dirt and rock slide which at one time appeared to have altered the course of this little stream.

Taking samples from the bedrock at the edge of the slide, I washed them carefully. The first two or three showed not a trace of gold, but the fourth pan produced two wheat-grain-sized nuggets. Several more pans finally brought forth another piece half the size of a match head.

"Not good," I told myself, "but it's a place to work if I don't find something better."

I tried a half dozen more pans without measurable success.

Nevertheless, next morning I went back to the ravine, this time armed with full-sized shovel and a sluice box about eight feet long which I had hurriedly hammered together from scrap lumber.

My plan was to dig a ditch to carry water around the hill above this small slide and wash the whole slide on through my sluice box. I didn't think I would find much gold, but I felt there was a chance I might hit some fairly heavy gold. Apparently the old-timers who had worked this section of the ravine had felt the little piece of ground was not worth working and simply had bypassed it.

The ditch would have to be about two hundred feet long and by noon I had the greatest part of it completed. The soil was soft and easy digging, and the ditch itself did not have to be more than a foot wide and seven or eight inches deep.

Carefully, I set the sluice at the lower end of the slide, wedged it with rocks, and then spaded a narrow cut from the end of my ditch through the soil to the sluice box so the water would follow this channel.

It is amazing how much earth a man can move in a day's time with this type of sluicing. The water does the work, and all the miner has to do is throw the larger rock out of the channel that the water cuts.

I was almost ready to start for the upper end of my ditch to turn the water into it when, suddenly, I was startled by a voice directly behind me.

"Just what the hell do you think you're doing here?"

I turned and found myself staring into the almost expressionless face of a stubble-bearded man who held a Winchester rifle in the crook of his arm.

I was so surprised I stammered. "I was just starting to do a little sniping here, I panned out a few colors yesterday, and I . . ."

"You Goddam snipers . . . you stay off my property, this is my mining claim," was the reply.

"Well, I'm sorry—I didn't see any location notice—I didn't think anyone would mind if I just scratched around here a little bit and tried to . . ."

The stubble-bearded man patted the rifle. "This is my location notice. And now you get the hell outa here and you stay out. And you tell all your sniper friends to stay out, too, unless somebody wants to get shot. I'm damn well tired of you two-bit prospectors snooping around here."

I gathered up pick, shovel, and pan and started down the ravine. When I looked back the man with the rifle was still there watching me.

Naturally, I told Dot about my experience when I got back to camp, and next day, when Big Tom happened to wander into camp on his way to town, I told him about it.

Tom laughed. "Well, you met Joe Thompson, did you. He doesn't care about the mining—he just doesn't like people. Used to be a bootlegger a few years back. He had a still hidden up there somewhere during Prohibition days and I guess he got so used to running people off his property he just can't break the habit."

I never saw Joe Thompson again, and I never went back up that ravine, either. As far as I know, my sluice box and that little piece of ground I was going to mine are there just as I left them.

CHAPTER III

CHRISTMAS ON THE AGUA FRIA

I AWAKENED THE SUNDAY MORNING BEFORE CHRISTMAS TO A steady patter of raindrops on our tenthouse roof.

It was early, and the interior of the tent still was shrouded in darkness. For a few minutes I lay there under the warm blankets listening to the rain, visualizing the cold, wet day that lay ahead of us out there on the creek where we would be sluicing.

Dot snuggled beside me, still sleeping soundly, and finally, summoning courage, I climbed from bed, pulled on my old Levi's and began rustling up a fire in the little stove.

There is one thing about a nine-by-twelve tenthouse, it warms up quickly, and by the time I had finished lacing my boots the coffeepot on the sheet-iron stove was bubbling merrily.

Ladybug came crawling out of her cardboard-box bed, yawning and stretching, and as usual, asked to be let outside to take care of her morning chores and to sniff carefully each inch of ground around our abode to determine what might have occurred there during the hours of darkness.

A few minutes later, just as the coffee finished perking, the dog barked to be let back in, and Dot began stirring to wakefulness.

I poured her a mug of coffee which she sipped slowly as she lay there in bed, listening throughtfully to the rain.

"Gonna get our butts wet out there today," I commented. "From the sounds of it and from the looks of those clouds, it's gonna rain all day."

Dot, who by now was dressing, paused for a moment. "Isn't this the day your dad and cousin Jack said they intended to come visit us—this is Sunday, isn't it?"

"Yes, this is Sunday. The Sunday before Christmas. I just plain forgot about it. This is the day they're to be here."

This sudden recollection threw a new light on the day's plans, and as Dot prepared the hotcake batter and began frying bacon we decided to stay in camp.

We were mining more than a mile upstream from our campsite and we both knew Dad and Jack would never find us there.

Dot decided this would be a good morning to clean house, and since our wood supply was getting a bit low, I decided to stay in camp and cut wood.

Shortly before noon, as I was splitting the last of a pretty fair sized pile of wood, there was a shout from up the trail, and into camp strode my dad and Jack.

The first thing I noticed, even before they got within actual speaking range, was that each of them carried a large, well-filled sack over his shoulders.

Hearing the shouts and the dog barking, Dot appeared at the tenthouse door. Dad greeted her with a kiss, a loud "Merry Christmas," and shoved the heavy sack into her hands.

The sack was so heavy Dot could hardly lift it, and the one that Jack was carrying was equally as large.

The sacks contained a dressed twenty-five-pound turkey, about a bushel of potatoes, oranges, apples, fresh vegetables, and a couple of big bags of almonds and walnuts.

"My Lord!" gasped Dorothy. "There's enough here to feed Jess and me all winter . . . You shouldn't have done it."

But a gift was a gift, and there was nothing to do but accept all that food and thank them for it.

Suddenly, we felt rich and Christmasy.

Lunch that day was a happy interlude. We talked and laughed a lot, and with considerable pride, showed them the gold we had mined.

But their stay was short, for about 2 P.M. the rain slacked off considerably, and Dad and Jack decided to take advantage of it and cover the two miles back up the trail to their car before another downpour started.

They started back up the trail, shouting "Merry Christmas" to us as they disappeared, and once again there was just the two of us and our little dog at our tent on the lonely Agua Fria.

We walked back inside the tenthouse, out of the drizzling rain, and looked again with awe at that huge pile of grub that was our Christmas present.

"Tell me," asked Dot, "when there isn't a pot or pan here big enough to cook a chicken, just how I am to go about roasting that twenty-five-pound dinosaur, and how two of us are going to eat it?"

But Dot is not a person who gives up easily.

"You know . . . I've got that big dishpan, and that turkey would fit into it. Now, if some other sniper along the river here had another dishpan the same size that would fit over the top, we could make a roaster, couldn't we?"

"Sure, we could," I replied. "And we could invite him to have Christmas dinner with us."

"Yes, but there's still more food here than three people could eat in a week, and I'd hate to see any of it spoil or go to waste," said Dorothy.

"You know," she said, "we could invite them all—all of the snipers along the river here—invite them to Christmas dinner with us."

"Sure we could. There must be nine or ten of them. There's old Jack, and Bill, and Big Tom and Sharkey, and the old-timer with the red whiskers. I'll bet every one of them would be damn glad to come."

Darkness was only a couple of hours away, and it was still raining, but I put on my old rain slicker and started up the river trail toward where a couple of the prospectors were camped.

It was well after dark by the time I returned home, but my mission, at least as far as I had gone, had met with total success.

Not only were the half-dozen fellows I had talked with enthusiastic about the idea, they were determined to help in any way they could.

Each would bring his own plate, knife, fork, and spoon, and they would supply gold pans to hold such things as mashed potatoes, giblet gravy, and vegetables.

Bill had a big dishpan exactly the same size as ours and he would willingly, in fact, he demanded that he be allowed to donate it to serve as the top of an improvised turkey roaster.

We would have to eat outside, because neither our tenthouse nor any of the other cabins or camps occupied by the snipers along the Agua Fria was large enough to seat more than two or three people at a time.

We finally ended up with thirteen persons who were asked to come to dinner.

"Thirteen," I said, "that's an unlucky number."

"Don't worry about it," said Dot. "If thirteen show up and anybody's superstitious, we'll just tie a dishtowel around Ladybug's neck and make her the fourteenth guest!"

Dot sat up late that night, working by the light of our tiny kerosene lamp, drawing up a menu that was to include pumpkin and mince pies, homemade bread, olives, cranberry sauce, stuffed celery, tossed salad, candied sweet potatoes, mashed potatoes and giblet gravey, and, of course, the centerpiece—twenty-five pounds of roast turkey with dressing.

By the time she had finished, her grocery list looked about as long as our sluice box and I was wondering if our meager cache of gold that sat in little bottles on the shelf would begin to cover even the most important items she had scribbled on her scratch pad.

"I'll simply do my best," I told myself, for I had never seen Dot look with more anticipation upon an event than she did toward this Christmas dinner she was planning.

I just could not summon the courage to tell her I didn't think we could afford all those things.

Some time during the night the drizzling rain stopped.

The sun was just starting to break over the ridgetops next morning and I was finishing my second cup of coffee and after-breakfast cigarette when Ladybug—who had just returned from her morning rounds—rushed to the door, barking.

Then I heard voices and the clump of heavy boots on the tenthouse steps.

"Anybody up around here this morning?"

I recognized Bill McCarty's voice and that of Big Tom. Red Whiskers was with them, and as I opened the door and they strode into the tenthouse, I could see they were dressed for town.

You could always tell when one of the snipers was headed for town because the overalls or Levi's he was wearing would have fewer patches than his work clothes.

His town jacket was generally a plaid mackinaw and he would be wearing laced leather boots.

His working jacket, if he wore one, was usually of faded, threadbare blue denim, and his footwear was gum boots.

Today the boys were slicked up in their town best.

"Thought you might need some help totin' those groceries from town," announced Bill, "so we decided we'd come along and give you a hand."

Dot divided the last of the coffee among them, and fifteen minutes later we took off up the trail for the top of the ridge where my old Chevvy was parked.

After only a nominal amount of cranking and cussing the Chevvy's old four-cylinder engine came to life and the four of us were bouncing and sliding down the rough, muddy, rain-slick dirt road.

Driving that road, which even in its best days had never seen the blade of a grader, was always an experience. In summer it was ankle deep in powdery red dust and in winter it was even deeper in mud.

This morning we were forced to stop twice to chop fallen trees which yesterday's wind and rainstorm had toppled across the road.

It was 10 A.M. by the time we reached the general store in Mariposa. The general store was the focal point of community life in Mariposa in those days.

Births, deaths, and marriages were announced on the store bulletin board. Here, all local gossip and news was exchanged.

You could buy potatoes or a new ax handle, a box of shotgun shells or a plow. If they did not have it they would get it.

Today the store was a beehive of activity. Ranchers were buying sacks of grain and housewives were stocking up for the Christmas holiday.

Little girls peeked around their mothers' skirts and small boys stood outside the hardware counter wishfully ogling the shining new guns and fishing tackle, piles of .22 shells, and the big Winchester calendar picture of the hunter facing the charging grizzly bear.

A lucky few of the youngsters clutched dripping ice cream cones in grubby hands.

Outside the store was the usual cluster of Indians stoically watching the goings-on.

Each of us snipers headed in a different direction to pick up various items that made up the shopping list.

The boys had added such items as Brazil and hazel nuts, some of the store's rock-hard Christmas candy "just because candy goes with Christmas," and another decided that a Christmas dinner demanded wine. Red Whiskers made sure that our list included after-dinner cigars and, luxury of luxuries, a pack of "tailor-made" Lucky Strikes for Dot.

Because my list was the longest, the boys finished their purchases first, and then went to the office of the store to cash in their gold dust.

I left my merchandise, every blessed thing that Dot had ordered, on the floor next to the counter and made my way to the back of the store where the office was located.

I still didn't know if I had enough dust to cover the cost of all that stuff, but I was going to cash it in and if there wasn't enough I was going to ask old Bert to trust me for the remainder until next week.

I shoved the little bottle of heavy yellow metal across the counter to him. He took it, looked at it quizzically, shook it back and forth, then set it down again.

"Sorry, Jess . . . I can't accept it; this stuff's no good."

For an instant I had a sort of sinking feeling down deep in my belly—and then I got mad!

"Why, dammit . . . that's as good a grade of gold as ever came into this store . . . it's pure, it's river gold right out of the Agua Fria—it's just like all the other gold I've always brought in here, and . . ."

Suddenly I realized that Bert was grinning from ear to ear.

"That's not exactly what I meant, Jess—what I mean to say is that this gold of yours can't buy anything in this store here today. Those boys that came in with you cashed their gold in just a few minutes ago and they left it with me. Told me that if I let you pay for one penny of the stuff you have out there they would kick hell out of me.

"And by the way, Java old boy, I got something here myself that you better take back to camp with you for that Christmas dinner."

Bert reached beneath the counter, brought out a fifth of brandy all done up in Christmas wrappings, and shoved it into my hands.

I just sort of stood there like a big dunce. I couldn't think of what to say and yet I wanted to say so much. I wanted to thank Bert and those boys waiting out there for me in the old Chevvy.

The whole world just seemed a hell of a lot nicer and a lot brighter as I picked up that big box of groceries and toted them to the car.

I knew only too well how hard every one of those fellows had worked for that gold they had cashed in and I knew that some of them might go a little bit hungry next week for what they had done today.

And, even the store owner—he sure wasn't getting rich in those Depression days in that little old crossroads store—yet he had handed me that bottle of brandy for which he had paid cold, hard cash. It was a pretty damned nice thing to have done.

By noon we were back in camp to find that the other boys along the river who had been invited to tomorrow's Christmas dinner had arrived to volunteer any help we might need.

It is amazing what a dozen men can accomplish in a couple of hours if they set their minds to it.

Among the first things we needed was a table.

Down the river a short distance from our camp was the remains of an old sheet-iron mine shack.

Two of the boys headed for the shack to bring back a piece of that four-by-eight sheet iron which would serve as a table top.

A couple of others grabbed my old cross-cut saw and headed for a dead pine snag that stood on the hill behind the tenthouse.

Four lengths of the old tree trunk served beautifully for table legs and they sawed another dozen short lengths to serve as seats.

They made firewood of the remainder of the old tree while others worked at building an outdoor fireplace on which Dot would do part of tomorrow's cooking.

But completion of our project was interrupted by Dot who stepped out of the tenthouse and began banging on a skillet with a large spoon.

On the newly completed table my wife set a steaming, black kettle of bacon and beans and a huge pan of hot cornbread.

Lunch finished, the gang insisted on cleaning up the table and washing the dishes themselves so that Dot could get back to pie making and other preparations for tomorrow's Christmas dinner.

By now it was midafternoon. One by one, the fellows thanked us, then began drifting back to their individual camps. With still some daylight left, most of them intended to do a little bit of sluicing before darkness fell. Each of them knew that the gold they mined each day would put beans in their bellies and clothes on their backs the next.

As I puttered around the outdoor fireplace, adding a finishing touch here and there, I could hear Dot singing to herself in the tenthouse as she went about her chores.

Suddenly, as I sat down to roll a cigarette in the quiet of the late afternoon, I realized—this was Christmas Eve.

Dot came out of the tenthouse, her hands still white with flour from the pie dough she had been making.

"I've done about all I can for now," she told me. "But we will have to get up awfully early in the morning so I can stuff the turkey and get started on the rest of the things. It will take seven or eight hours to roast that turkey."

I rolled her a cigarette—she never could really get the knack of rolling a homemade cigarette herself, and her attempts usually resulted in nothing but wastage of good Bull Durham.

The sun was well down by now, its last rays just faintly touching the ridgetops high above us, but the air, even though it was December 24, was warm, carrying almost the balminess of spring.

"Do you realize," I asked, "what tonight is—that this is Christmas Eve? And I haven't even gotten you a Christmas present—haven't even taken time out to get a Christmas tree . . ."

Dorothy took a drag on her cigarette.

"I don't care about the Christmas present—and if we want one—we can get a Christmas tree tomorrow. I still think this is going to be one of the nicest Christmases we've ever had."

I awakened Christmas morning to find Dot up and dressed, busily stuffing the huge turkey.

Outdoors it was still totally dark, and even after I dressed and drank my coffee it was still almost too dark to see the path to the river when Dot asked me to get her a fresh bucket of water.

But a half hour later I heaved a sigh of relief as the sun peeked over the hill, heralding a clear day.

By that time I had the fire going in the outdoor fireplace, and moments later, Dot and I carefully set our double dishpan roaster containing twenty-five pounds of stuffed turkey, over the glowing coals.

Midmorning rolled around and the first of our eleven dinner guests arrived.

Big Tom was among the early arrivals, and with him came the Christmas tree.

The tree, a perfectly formed little Douglas fir about three feet tall, was already decorated.

The decorations included the natural brown little fir cones, little silver bells fashioned from the tinfoil of cigarette packs, and stars painstakingly cut from the tops of tin cans.

Sharkey came striding up the river trail with a gallon of wine with which to toast our Christmas.

True, it was only muscatel—snipers' champagne he called it—and our wine glasses included tin cups, jelly glasses, and several of those little tin cans that tomato sauce comes in.

The men sat around the fire on the pine blocks that served as chairs, sipped their wine, swapped lies, and took turns helping Dorothy prepare dinner.

The mouth-watering aroma of roasting turkey drifted from the big dishpans as they peeled spuds, cleaned Brussels sprouts and celery, pared apples and cracked walnuts for apple and walnut (Waldorf) salad.

Noon rolled around, then 1 P.M., and finally at 2 P.M. Dorothy announced the turkey ready for carving.

Using my old hunting knife, I did the honors while Dot finished the giblet gravy that was served in a gold pan.

There were cans of olives and jars of pickles, fluffy mashed potatoes and candied yams, Brussels sprouts, and canned asparagus tips.

And crowning the whole great array of food was that huge twenty-five-pound turkey with great mounds of rich, hot dressing.

Little "Shorty" Hargraves, whom I later learned had studied for the priesthood, bowed his head and quietly offered grace.

For these eleven men grouped around us, most of whom had not sat down to a woman's cooking or a meal like this in longer than they cared to remember, it was a solemn moment.

Each sat there at the table, perhaps a little embarrassed, each for a moment lost in his own thoughts of other places and other Christmases.

"Well, don't just sit there," I finally said. "Dig in, you fellas, before this grub gets cold."

If it was surprising to see what that dozen men could do in the line of work when they set their minds to it, you should see what that same dozen could do to a pile of food and a twenty-five-pound turkey when they put their appetites to the task.

Halfway through the meal, with a drumstick clutched in one hand and a big forkful of mashed potatoes in the other, Big Tom paused just long enough to look up and comment:

"By gad, Jess! That wife of yours is the best cook west of the damn Rockies—and probably east of 'em, too!"

There was a chorus of assent from around the table, and the praise was so loud and long it embarrassed poor Dot.

Finally, we were down to dessert—mince and pumpkin pies, coffee laced with brandy—and Red Whiskers passed out the cigars.

With considerable ceremony, Dorothy was presented with her pack of Lucky Strikes and I was threatened with dire consequence if I smoked even one of them.

Dinner completed, all eleven of our guests pitched into the clean-up job.

They washed and polished pots and pans until they shone, cleaned up the table, and insisted that any leftover food remain with us.

But it was still pretty early and each was loath to leave the companionship that radiated around our little campfire.

We sat there smoking and spinning yarns, gold strikes we or someone else had made, or strikes we someday hoped to make.

Bill McCarty, a normally calm, phlegmatic man who toiled each day on a little gravel bar a couple miles up the river to make his fifty cents or a dollar, spun a tale of a rich spot up on Yellow Jacket Canyon which both the 49ers and the Chinamen had missed.

"Rough spot to get into," explained McCarty.

"An ancient slide covered the old river channel. Some of the boulders in the slide were as big as that tent. It was rich, but the old-timers—the 49ers—were always in a hurry and those boulders made the mining awfully difficult. There was good ground up ahead, so they just bypassed it.

"The Chinamen," McCarty went on, "came into the county in the late fifties or early sixties and started to work it, cubby-holing in among those boulders. They were making good money.

"But an old-timer who said he had a claim on the slide ran 'em off—took a shotgun to 'em, and I guess he killed a couple. Anyway, the Chinese pulled out—never worked it. The old man with the shotgun was working another spot and meanwhile the coyote holes the Chinese dug into the slide caved over at the mouth.

"Well, the old boy died before he ever got to working the slide and his mining claim lapsed, and nobody bothered to investigate it again.

"Four years ago—back in '33—my partner and I got digging around there and opened up one of those little drifts the Chinamen had run. Funny thing, after we got the mouth of that little tunnel mucked out we found it was still open enough to crawl into.

"We got back in there, and in three days we took out one hundred and twenty-five dollars in coarse gold.

"But that was in November, and a big storm came up—real heavy rain. It raised the water level of the canyon and water poured into the tunnel.

"We knew we wouldn't be able to get back into it until spring, so we broke camp and pulled out. Went down on the American River for the winter.

"Well, next spring my partner got sick and finally went into a Veterans Hospital down around the Bay someplace. There I was alone, and I didn't want to tackle that Yellow Jacket country by myself . . . Far as I know, that slide is still there with that little tunnel in it, and I tell you fellas, it's rich as blue blazes! One of these days I'm going back."

Stories like that went on all afternoon.

Evening came and we ate again, just picking at the remains of the turkey and the other stuff.

The brandy bottle was empty and coffee just about gone when the last of the snipers finally said his goodbyes and headed out along the river trail for his lonely camp.

About all that was left of the turkey were some bones that would make a snack for Ladybug.

Alone again—just the two of us—I poured Dorothy and myself each a last cup of coffee as we sat beside the dying fire.

Dorothy lit one of her precious tailor-made cigarettes, took a deep drag and a sip of coffee.

"You know, Jess, I think this has been the best, the most heartwarming Christmas I've ever had."

CHAPTER IV

GOLD IS WHERE YOU FIND IT

THE OLD SAYING "GOLD IS WHERE YOU FIND IT" MAY BE TRUE, BUT it helps to beat hell if you have an idea where to look.

Our first winter and spring on the Agua Fria did not see us exactly overcome with wealth, but, day by day we eked out a living, working spots here and there which the old-timers, the Chinamen, and generations of snipers who followed them had missed or given up on because of meager returns.

We probably averaged about a dollar a day, once in a while hitting a sweet spot, but there were other times when a hard day's work netted little more than fifty cents.

But we survived. And as we came to know the country better and improved our mining techniques our average increased a bit.

There was one thing I quickly learned. The easy spots had been worked out, and those early-day miners were just as smart and every bit as ambitious as we were.

One time we worked for three days moving rocks and cubby-holing under a huge boulder where I was sure we would hit a piece of virgin ground. I finally got beneath the boulder only to find remnants of solid oak logs some long-forgotten miner had used for shoring while he scraped the gravel from beneath it. Our total take for that three days' work was less than a couple dollars.

Yet we did find spots other miners had missed. I learned to look for the unlikely places, and while an awful lot of them didn't pay off, now and then we would hit something good.

One frosty January morning while on our way up the river trail to a gravel bar we had been working with only limited success, Dot paused for a moment to retie a boot lace which had come loose. As I stood waiting for her I noticed a little bench of rough, broken slate rock over which flowed a tiny tributary rill of the main stream.

Really, without much purpose in mind, I walked over to the exposed slate, and as I did, I noticed a thin piece which through freezing and thawing, had loosened to the point I could easily lift it with my fingers from the other more tightly held layers of rock. Plastered on the side of the little slab of rock which was less than a half-inch thick and about the size of my hand, was a thin layer of yellow, clayish-looking silt. I was carrying no tools, but using the blade of my pocket knife, I managed to pry loose another piece of slate about the same size.

I certainly was not excited, but I was interested. I knew this particular spot certainly had been worked over many times. Piles of rock stacked on each side of the little rill were clear evidence that it once had been covered with gravel and had certainly been mined.

"Why don't you just sit here and wait for me while I go on up to the sluice box and get a pick and a gold pan," I told Dot, who had finished tying her boot and had walked over to see what I was doing.

Twenty minutes later I was back with gold pan, a sharp pick, and a small crevicing tool.

Carefully, I broke out chunks of slate with the pick, prying each one loose and cleaning it in the gold pan. Each piece had a layer of mud- and clay-congealed silt on one side of it. It took fifteen minutes before I managed to accumulate a double handful of the fine silt, and wondering whether it contained even a few colors, I walked down to the edge of the stream and began the miserable job of panning in that ice-cold river water.

But even before half of the fine dirt was washed from the pan I saw the first colors, tiny grains of gold like coarse cornmeal, and some larger. And the string of gold in the pan became longer each time I swirled it in the clear, cold water. I washed away the last bit of sandy residue, and there, wet and glistening in the morning sun, was at least three dollars' worth of fine gold.

Before the day was out we had worked that entire little bench. That night in the tenthouse, by the light of the kerosene lamp, I dumped the heap of yellow grains onto the gold scales. They weighed just $76.20.

And while $76 may not seem like any fortune, for Dot and me it was the difference between just barely scraping along on a starvation diet and being able to buy the food we needed and the warm clothes and other necessities for a decent living.

Nor were we the only ones who sometimes lucked out there on the Agua Fria during those hungry, Depression days.

Bill McCarty had a penchant for exploring old mine tunnels, shafts, or any other kind of diggings that some long-forgotten miner had coyote-holed into the ground. About all he ever had gotten for his efforts were a collection of scratches, bruises, and torn and muddy clothes. But if a man persists long enough, sometimes the odds lean his way.

One evening after supper Ladybug's barking and the thump of heavy boots on the tenthouse steps heralded the arrival of a visitor, and when I opened the door in strode Bill McCarty.

His eyes were sparkling with excitement and his face was split with a grin that ran from ear to ear.

"Jess, God damn it . . . Take a look at this!" In his hand Bill carried a small canvas sack, and before I could even reply or question him, he dumped its contents on our oilcloth-topped table.

Chunks of white quartz, each literally shot with gold, spilled into the lamplight, glistening rich and yellow. "Ohhh my gosh . . . look at that," Dot cried, almost dropping the plate she had been drying. There were three large pieces, about the size of a pack of cigarettes, and several smaller pieces, ranging down to the size of marbles. Each was at least a third raw gold and I knew that we had before us at least several hundred dollars.

"Found it this afternoon. Just stumbled onto it in an old prospect hole. I dug the first chunk out with my knife and an old piece of dull, rusty drill steel I found lying on the edge of the hole. I beat it back to camp and got a pick and shovel, by that time it was getting dark. I got this much and had to quit."

What puzzled me at first was why Bill would be prospecting without a pick or shovel, but as he calmed down a bit, the story came out.

Bill, who had been sluicing down on the river as the rest of us had been doing, knocked off work at noon that day to do a bit of necessary hunting. Taking his rifle, Bill climbed the ridge between the Agua Fria and Slug Gulch and began slowly working his way along the west slope in hope of jumping a deer.

About midafternoon a buck got up out of a little patch of chemise brush, and with a lucky shot Bill knocked him down. He walked the hundred yards to the fallen deer, dressed it out, and was getting ready to shoulder his load and head back to camp when a few yards away he noticed some chunks of exposed quartz rock. Closer examination showed the rock to be lying on the edge of a prospect hole about seven or eight feet deep.

Bill climbed down into the hole, poked around awhile and found nothing, although the quartz rock was heavily iron-stained, and had indications that it might carry gold.

Finally, tiring of his project, Bill started to climb back out, but noticed one corner of the little shaft was especially crumbled, broken, and brown with rusty-colored iron stain.

Pulling out his still bloody pocket knife, Bill probed the broken rock, easily tumbling out small chunks. Then, to his utter amazement, a walnut-sized piece of quartz broke loose and Bill could hardly believe his eyes. The rock was almost half gold!

"I tell ya, I had to pinch myself to make sure I wasn't dreaming," said Bill, his ruddy face fairly glowing.

"That prospector—whoever he was—just plain dug right past the pocket, missed it by inches as he went down following a little trace of gold," said Bill. "I'm goin' up there again tomorrow, as soon as it gets daylight."

It was almost dark the next evening when Bill came striding down the trail past our camp. I was out getting an armful of wood, and naturally I hollered at him to find out how he had done.

"Well, not too bad, Java, course it wasn't quite as good as I hoped, but look at this." From his little sack Bill tumbled several marble-sized pieces of quartz that showed gold. He also had a small bottle with perhaps a half ounce of finer gold in it.

"She sorta petered out on me this afternoon," Bill admitted, "but I know there's more there. Only thing is, that rock has tightened up, and I'm going to have to drill and blast."

Bill spent the next day sharpening some drill steel, then went into town and bought half a box of dynamite.

For two weeks Bill worked in his quartz mine, leaving camp at daylight, returning at dark, but hardly another color of gold did he find. He finally gave up and went back to sluicing gravel on the river.

But for Bill, it was still a pretty profitable two weeks, he sold the gold taken from the prospect hole for just a bit better than five hundred dollars.

It was not unusual during the 1930s for men to wander across really big strikes.

During the fall stories drifted along the Mother Lode about a huge gold strike up on the American River where the government was building a dam.

Like most rumors of gold strikes, we discounted them about 90 percent. Then, a former resident of Mariposa who had been working on the project came home because the job had closed down, and told us the true story.

The dam project was located on the American River east of Auburn at a spot called Rucky Chucky, on the edge of what, historically, had been a rich pocket mining area.

Late one afternoon a bulldozer operator was sent up the hill a hundred yards above the damsite to level a spot for an electrical transformer station.

As he dug into the side hill at exactly the spot where the old river trail, traveled nearly a century ago by miners, crossed the damsite, the catskinner began unearthing chunks of quartz rock. Being something of a mining man, he climbed off his rig to inspect the quartz, and found it was loaded with gold.

The next minute he was shouting and waving his hat, and other workmen came running.

The discovery triggered a stampede. Workers dropped their tools and began digging into the hillside.

The end result was that the dam project actually came to a halt. The men formed some sort of a loose knit company and over loud protests of the contracting company and the federal government, they went to mining.

In the space of two or three weeks more than $100,000 in raw gold was taken out by the workmen while the dam project lay idle.

The gold was supposed to have been put into a common pool and equally divided, but from what we heard, as much gold was stolen as was ever put into the pool.

Later that year because of faulty geological formations and a huge rock slide, the dam project was abandoned. But for years afterward, snipers and prospectors prowled the area still picking up a few colors and trying to find another pocket like the one the catskinner hit.

Late winter came, and heavy rains raised the level of the Agua Fria until most of the gravel bars and worthwhile bedrock along the river's edge were unworkable.

One morning we were prospecting for a new place to mine when we wandered across the little flat where the old gold rush town of Agua Fria had stood. We had crossed it many times before, for the river trail went right through the middle of it. There were remnants of old foundations, and in a couple of places, overgrown with brush and weeds, piles of stone which had once been fireplaces.

One large foundation, outlined by pieces of flat, heavy stone, lay nearest the river, and it was there I sat down to roll a cigarette.

As I sat enjoying my smoke and watching the river, Dot prowled around the old foundation, now and then picking up a rusty square nail or bit of broken, rusty metal.

I finished the cigarette, stubbed it out and was just getting to my feet when Dot suddenly called to me. "Jess—look here at what I just found." She was on her knees in the soft, sandy loam, and in the palm of her hand she held a tarnished but perfect Indian head penny. It had been minted in 1862.

"This foundation is so big I'll bet it was an old store," said Dot. "Do you suppose that coin is worth anything?"

"Well, it's worth at least a penny," I told her, "but this gives me an idea. If this was a store that dates back to when this place was a town, there probably was considerable gold dust changed hands in it. Some of it might have gotten lost or spilled."

I pulled a gold pan out of my pack and scooped it full of the soft, charcoal-studded soil. A few minutes later the load of dirt was reduced to only a bit of residual sand in the bottom of the pan and with the sand was about ten cents in fine gold.

"Hey, this is all right, if we can average this much a pan it's worth working." I tried a second pan in another spot, and came up with only a trace of color, but a third pan produced at least another ten cents.

Both of us spent the rest of the morning panning, and almost every pan showed color. It was good enough to actually work, we decided, so that afternoon I went back to camp and brought up the pump and a sluice box.

We skimmed the dirt down to the depth of about eight inches or more, working the entire area within the square of foundation rocks. It was easy digging because the dirt was soft, and it washed through the sluice box quickly, with only a minimum of rocks to remove. The one thing we had to be carcful of was broken glass, for the ground inside the foundation was littered with it.

In addition we found a horde of other odds and ends ranging from tiny perfume bottles to parts of old lamps, spoons, pieces of cheap jewelry and earrings, old whiskey bottles, and the remains of a badly rusted and burned derringer.

In gold dust we averaged about four dollars per day, but on the second day we came up with more than a dozen coins, including two five-dollar goldpieces, a couple of silver dollars, and numerous pennies.

The second day and the third day of cleaning up the foundation of the old store added more coins, until we had forty-eight of them in all, mostly pennies and quarters. Virtually all of the silver coins were at least partially melted. In one corner we found a curious conglomeration of melted coins which apparently had been in a cigar box or purse when the building burned. These coins, actually welded together by heat, appeared to be three silver dollars, five half-dollars, a ten-dollar goldpiece, and four quarters.

For years, after we quit mining and moved to San Andreas, I kept that stack of melted coins on our fireplace mantel in the living room as a conversation piece.

One day, a couple years ago, I suddenly noticed they had disappeared. Someone apparently had pocketed them, feeling they needed them worse than we did.

On the final day of work in the old foundation as I shoveled a load of dirt into the sluice box, Dot let out a squawk and made a grab at the riffles.

There, lying in the wet sand were two quarters, a dime, and a little nugget worth about a dollar.

It was twenty-seven years later when I found out what those two quarters and that dime were worth. I sold the two quarters for a thousand dollars, and the dime, which I still have in our safe deposit box, is valued at five hundred. Since then I have called that my $1501 shovelful.

At the end of the fourth day we had the foundation completely cleaned, and our take consisted of about twenty dollars' worth of gold, plus the coins.

Next day we drove into town, cashed the gold at the store, and showed off the coins. Naturally, everyone was interested in where we had found them, and I explained as best I could the location of the old store.

Old "Uncle Billy" Gibson, who was among the interested spectators, snorted: "Store, hell!—I remember that place—that was the old whorehouse!"

That night when we were back at the tenthouse Dot was again inspecting the perfect two quarters and the dime before she put them away.

She turned, looked at me, and grinned. "Jess Coffey . . . if you don't want to get shot you just better not start telling people that I earned this money working in a bawdy house!"

Sunday morning was usually the morning Dot did the weekly washing and I chopped wood. She used a tin washtub and a scrubboard which I dubbed "the Irish piano," and then rinsed the suds-filled clothes in the clear water of the creek.

The rinsing always took place each time at the same spot, a large, flat piece of clean bedrock at the edge of a pool. Often, instead of using a clothesline, Dot simply spread the clothes on the clean, sun-warmed bedrock to dry.

On this particular morning Dot already had washed, rinsed, and spread the clothes to dry, and had returned an hour or so later to gather them up when I heard her yell.

"Hey, Jess, come down here and bring a gold pan, will you!"

Wondering what the heck she needed with a gold pan when washing clothes, I lay down my ax, sauntered over to the tent-house and picked up an extra pan.

Dot was kneeling there at the river's edge, digging with her fingers in a small sand- and gravel-filled pothole near where the drying clothes lay.

"Look here," she said. "I was just poking in this little hole, waiting for a couple of your shirts to completely dry, and I found this." In the palm of her hand she held a tiny nugget about the size of a bead.

"Here, give me that pan." She grabbed the gold pan, scooped the little pile of fine gravel into it—there was less than a single panful—and a moment later she was busily washing it. Then, Dot really let out a yell!

There, shining in the bottom of the pan was a beautiful little five-dollar nugget and several more wheat-sized pieces of gold. In just ten minutes she had found more than eight dollars' worth of gold—in a tiny pothole over which she had been walking for more than a year.

But finding isn't always getting. An elderly man and his son moved onto the river and set up camp not far from Red Whiskers's cabin. They puttered along, up and down the river for several weeks with gold pan and sluice box, barely making enough to eat on. Then, one day at a spot not more than seventy-five yards from Red Whiskers's cabin, they moved some gravel and came upon a deep crevice that began to pay pretty good.

For a couple of days father and son worked diligently, and, according to Red Whiskers, took out more than an ounce of fairly coarse gold. But the crevice narrowed and got deeper, and even with thin, steel-crevicing tools they could not reach the bottom of it. Someone of the various snipers who happened by their workings suggested they drill a hole, put in a stick of dynamite and crack the bedrock to reach the bottom of the crevice. It sounded like a good idea.

Bill McCarty loaned the men a couple of sharp drills and a sledgehammer, and being generous, gave them a half dozen sticks of dynamite left over from his quartz mining operation.

The old man and his son spent most of the next day drilling a hole about three feet deep in the hard bedrock alongside the crevice, and it was late afternoon by the time they were ready to set off their blast.

Red Whiskers already had returned from work and was cooking supper. Dot, who was on her way back to camp from where she and I had been working that day, arrived on the scene just about the time the old man and his boy were ready to light the fuse.

Naturally, she had to stay for the excitement, but what she didn't know was that the men instead of using a single stick of dynamite had loaded into the hole all six sticks Bill had given them.

The younger of the two men lit the fuse, it spat its little train of fire, and then blue smoke began to curl into the air as it burned slowly toward the charge. The men scurried some forty yards up the trail from the crevice, Dot along with them, and stood waiting tensely for the blast.

"Do you think we're far enough away," asked Dot.

"Oh sure—it's just going to be a little pop. —I've handled powder all my life," replied the older of the two men.

Suddenly the air was split with a blast that shook the pine trees. Chunks of rock erupted and sailed for a hundred yards or more in every direction. A chunk sailed past Dot's head, missing her by inches. Another smaller piece hit the old man on the leg, tearing his pants and inflicting a nasty bruise. Several chunks rained down on the roof of Red Whiskers's cabin, and one, the size of a large baseball, went right through the shingles, bounced off the stove and upset his frying pan.

Red Whiskers came flying out of his cabin door, waving the still hot frying pan he had retrieved from the floor, trying to curse in two languages at once.

"Vot de hell iss going on out here . . . Who iss going to veex my cabin roof . . ."

The old man was sitting down holding his leg and his son stood there looking as if he wanted to run.

As for the crevice, all there was left was a gaping hole in the bedrock where the crevice had been. Any gold it might have contained was scattered over a quarter-mile of creek and hillside.

Next day the dynamite expert and his son broke camp and left Mariposa County.

CHAPTER V

THEY WERE CHARACTERS ALL

MOST OF THE PEOPLE WE FIRST MET WERE NEWCOMERS TO THE country like ourselves, snipers driven to the mountains and to mining by the Depression.

But, gradually, as we became established our circle of friends and acquaintances widened to include many of the natives and older, permanent residents of the area around Mariposa.

If there was one thing to be said of those who had lived their lives in these foothills it was that they were an individualistic and highly independent breed. They had cockleburred themselves to the land and had held on through good times and bad. They complained that the country was going to hell—that there was no work, that ranching was slow starvation and the mining was all gone—but you couldn't have run one of those old natives out of the country with a shotgun.

Although they had much in common in many ways, each had developed his own characteristics and traits which made him as different from the other as chickens are from ducks.

Among the old-timers there were friendships and enmities cemented over a lifetime, and seldom was there a very wide strip of middle ground. Some who had known and associated with each other since schooldays would not even offer a grunt of recognition as they met on the way to the post office to pick up the afternoon mail.

Others, old cronies who had drunk and brawled and worked together all their lives, now spent long summer afternoons holding down the liar's bench on the hotel porch or in front of the general store. And, although they were friends of long-standing, each thought of himself as the only true authority on early day happenings and history of the area. And each, behind the other's back would deride the other's stories, generally summing them up as "all a pack of damned lies."

Honesty in all things—except perhaps in the spinning of tales or recounting of recent events noteworthy of rehashing—was highly prized, and by far, the great majority of the people we met and dealt with were persons to respect and remember. But not all of the characters were old-timers, and not all of them were ringed with the halo of honesty or righteousness.

"Old Cap" was neither newcomer nor old-timer, but had wandered into the country some time during the 1920s and took up residence in an abandoned shack on a branch of Agua Fria Creek a couple miles from where we were camped.

Cap actually was not old—somewhere in his forties I would guess. He was a big man, bald headed and somewhat paunchy, who had gained his nickname from the old Salvation Army cap and coat he habitually wore winter and summer.

A packrat among other things, Cap's run-down shanty was surrounded with odds and ends of junk lugged home from everywhere within a ten-mile radius. Nor was Cap too particular about how he acquired his assortment which ranged from old washtubs to empty wine bottles, broken tools and rusty mining equipment and old mowing-machine parts. If a sniper returned to his diggings to find pick, shovel, or other tools missing, chances were a trip to Cap's litter-strewn premises would result in their recovery.

Cap was always effusely apologetic. "Didn't know who they belonged to—thought some sniper probably had given up and pulled out, just left his stuff there—didn't want to see somebody come along and steal it."

Cap was never known for his industriousness, and at first Dot and I were puzzled when we heard other miners and townspeople refer to him as "the 90 percent miner."

But it didn't take long to find out the meaning of the term. Cap had a habit of approaching newcomers when they arrived on the Agua Fria and propositioning them to go partners with him in a mining operation.

A lot of the men, green at the mining game, were only too willing to take on a partner who not only was experienced, but who told them he had located a rich little spot just about right for two men to work. The partnership operation went something like this, Cap always handled the sluice box and dip can while his partner did the shovel work.

Furthermore, while the partner did 90 percent of the work, Cap, it usually turned out, got about 90 percent of the pay. Cap's partners often spoke in puzzled fashion of the fact that while other miners quite often in a day's work found small nuggets worth two-bits or fifty cents, they and Cap never recovered anything but fine gold.

The truth was, that whenever Cap, tending the sluice box, saw in the riffles any flash of color bigger than a match head he simply waited until his partner's back was turned and the little nugget disappeared into his coat pocket.

One day Dot and I were eating lunch beside our sluice box when a young man who was mining with Cap came striding down the creek trail toward us. We invited him to have a cup of coffee and asked why he and Cap were not mining.

Cap had gotten sick and gone home, the fellow said. Seems as though Cap had left him moving boulders and had walked up a little side gully from the main creek to do some sample panning. A short time later, said Cap's partner, Cap returned, complained of not feeling well, and suggested they shut down for the day while he went home to recover from his sudden illness.

"Illness, hell," I snorted. "I'll bet you the best nugget I find all week the old devil hit something good he doesn't want to share. He's using that story of a belly ache to get away from you."

Sure enough, a few days later when we went into town for groceries we heard at the store that Cap had cashed a twelve-dollar nugget and had been drunk on wine for three days.

Not long after that Cap tried a similar trick on another partner and was two weeks recuperating from the bruises and the pair of black eyes he had accumulated as a result of it.

But Cap didn't learn easy. Shortly before we left the Agua Fria a sniper who lived down the river from us a mile or so had to make a trip back down to the city for a few days.

Knowing all too well old Cap's tendencies toward easy acquisition, this miner took such items as food, his rifle, and other small belongings, and left them at a neighboring prospector's camp.

The miner returned three or four days later, and his first stop was at his friend's camp to pick up the various articles and his gun he had left for safekeeping. He started down the trail to his own camp, arriving just in time to catch Cap in the act of walking away with a load of tools, blankets, and other equipment.

They spotted each other at about the same instant, but Cap was the first to react. He dropped his armload of plunder and took off for the brush.

Either Cap was lucky or the camp owner was the world's worst shot, for the next moment the air was full of whistling rifle slugs. For a big man, they said Cap did a masterful job of covering ground, but just as he was about a jump short of the brushline a bullet caught his boot right at the point of the heel. The slug tore the heel off the boot and split the sole of his boot right down the middle, inflicting only a minor scratch along the bottom of his callused foot.

Within hours the story spread to every camp along the river and had reached town.

Next day when Cap came limping into the general store and

asked for a new pair of boots the town convulsed with laughter. And, for weeks after, the town wags and the members of the liar's bench would go out of their way to ask Cap if he had found any abandoned camps lately.

In addition to miners such as Bill McCarty, Big Tom, Red Whiskers, and Sharkey whom we saw almost every day, and who became our close friends, there were many others scattered in camps and cabins up and down the river.

There was Charlie Dawson, who although a successful sniper when he worked for himself, spent so much time helping others that he was continually on the brink of destitution.

Charlie would give you the shirt off his back. Just mention that you had a big boulder to move or there was a log in the way of your mining operation, and Charlie would drop his own work to help you move it. If you happened to be chopping wood around camp and Charlie came along, headed for town, he was more apt than not to take off his jacket, grab a spare ax if you had one, and spend the rest of the day helping you.

Then, there was Pete, lecherous and liquorous, who had a succession of women living with him. The women, usually refugees from Merced, Fresno, or Stockton skid rows, never stayed long, for the rosy picture Pete painted of his mountain retreat didn't quite turn out to be what he promised when they saw it in reality. They usually left at about the time the liquor ran out.

One of them, however, before taking leave grabbed a butcher knife and tried to carve her initials on Pete's hide. He carried a scar that ran from ear to chin, but it apparently did little to cool his ardor for feminine companionship, for when we left the Agua Fria he was living with another new import from one of the valley towns.

Down near the mouth of Slug Gulch lived an old-timer I knew only as "Vince," who worked a little quartz mine up on the mountain.

Industrious, and frugal, Vince spent no hard-earned money

on clothes or household frills. His cabin was a one-room shack, his clothes ragged, faded tatters, yet on several occasions he showed me specimens of gold that I know weighed several ounces each, and were worth well over a hundred dollars.

Vince slept in his cabin but cooked outdoors, and his only cooking implement was a frying pan. One day when I was prospecting Slug Gulch I arrived at his camp just at noon.

"Hello, Jess," he greeted me, "you're just in time for grub."

Grub in this case was boiled potatoes which Vince was slicing with a grimy-looking jackknife, and some slabs of salt pork. He had a fire of manzanita coals burning in his outdoor fireplace.

I suddenly noticed the frying pan, a big cast-iron skillet leaning against the bole of an oak tree a few feet from the fire. A line of large red ants was parading into one side of the skillet and out the other, each carrying a bit of food left from whatever Vince had cooked for breakfast. A few luckless ones struggled valiantly to free themselves from pools of congealed grease in which they had become trapped.

Vince grabbed the frying pan, thumped it upside down against a rock a couple of times to oust the excess ants, then popped it onto the fire. A few remaining fried ants sputtered in the grease as Vince dumped in the potatoes, and I, somewhere during that interval, had lost my appetite. I settled for a cup of coffee from a not too clean cup and went on my way.

Shortly after arriving in the gold country we met "Uncle Billy" Gibson, who although not a 49er, had arrived in the California gold fields at the age of fourteen, in 1861.

Uncle Billy was a bachelor, and at eighty-six was still spry and agile, with surprisingly sharp mind. According to his own stories, and to the tales of other old-timers who knew him, Uncle Billy had made and lost at least two fortunes in the mining game.

Back in the 1870s when hydraulic mining was in its heydey, when miners with giant hydraulic nozzles were virtually washing away whole mountains in their quest for gold, Uncle

Billy and his partners hit a rich diggings on one of the forks of the American River.

Water enough for hydraulicking was a problem at that particular location, and they could mine only during the winter months. But December through March, according to the old man—and I believe him—he and his partners averaged three hundred dollars a day.

They shut down their mining operation in April when their water supply gave out and took a stagecoach to San Francisco to cash in their gold at the United States Mint.

Each rented a suite in a San Francisco hotel, visited the best tailors in town, then set out to see the bright lights.

One version of Billy's San Francisco escapades, told to me by another old-timer who should have known, is that one night he and one of his partners rented an entire parlor house, then invited in friends to share its drinks and other entertainment with them.

In an expansive mood one day, Uncle Billy got to reminiscing and recalled that one year after his annual trip to San Francisco, he had to borrow money to live on until the next hydraulic mining season started.

In later years Billy discovered a quartz mine from which he took several good-sized pockets, and then later sold the property for ten thousand dollars.

The new owners of the mine developed it, and in the space of a few years took out nearly a million dollars.

When I knew him, Uncle Billy lived in a one-room cabin, not far from town, and his entire income was a small, monthly old-age pension check. I visited him from time to time, for he still had a tremendous knowledge of mining, and he knew spots of ground still worth working.

Uncle Billy hated to cut wood. He cut it a stick at a time, and used it frugally.

The last time I ever visited the old man was a cold, blustery February day. He was sitting in a chair hunched beside his little wood stove, wearing a heavy sweater, and the oven door of the stove was open in order to obtain maximum warmth from the tiny fire he had burning.

In fact, the fire in the stove was so low, and the cabin so cold, that Uncle Billy's cat was curled up in the oven in order to keep warm.

During the 1930s the mining country along the Mother Lode was sporadically invaded by mining promoters—men who most generally were working on someone else's money—or hoping to interest someone with money in one kind of mining scheme or another. They were not half so interested in the gold in the ground as in the money in some financial backer's pocket. It was these men, fly-by-nighters who leased worthless properties, established bogus mines, and ended up fleecing innocent investors, who gave gold mine development a generally bad name.

A big, blustery man called "Skip" who made it known he was a mining property developer moved into the country and started talking pretty big about leasing mining ground. He drove a big car, ran up a big bill at the hotel, and wearing Stetson and engineer's boots, toured the country looking at mines and talking mining, but no money changed hands. It took no great length of time for the local people to tag this newcomer as a blowhard who drank too much, talked too much, and, when drunk, engaged in fights at the drop of a hat.

Then Skip really began making himself unpopular. He appeared one morning on the Agua Fria, wearing his fancy clothes, and began staking out mining claims along the river. He was bringing in a mining company to dredge the stream for gold, he said, and forthwith served notice that all snipers living and working on the claims he staked would have to move out immediately. Later, in a more magnanimous moment, he announced that those who wished to stay for the time being could pay him rent or a part of their profits.

At first, this fellow had us pretty worried. In fact, Dot and I and several others with neither means nor intentions of paying rent or a share of our hard-won earnings from the river began making plans to move.

The situation dragged on for a couple of weeks with threats and blustering from Skip, as he marked out more claims and got into several hot and heavy name-calling arguments with permanent residents on whose land he infringed.

Then, Shorty Hargraves arrived from town one afternoon with news that changed the picture considerably. Skip, he told us, might be staking out lots of claims, but he had not recorded a single one of them in the Mariposa County Courthouse. The claims were completely invalid.

But Skip, apparently unaware that we had discovered his claims were not legal, continued to threaten various snipers with suit, eviction, and bodily harm if they did not get off his property or pay rent. His first open brush with one of the snipers we knew was with Big Bill McCarty—and on Skip's part, it was a poor choice.

Bill was every bit as big as Skip, and he was lean and hardened from long days of labor on the river.

It was midafternoon when Skip, about half drunk, approached the spot where McCarty was busy sluicing.

"Well," he announced, "I haven't seen any rent coming in from you and I guess you know you're working on my mining claim. I've got some mining men coming in here in a few days to look over this ground, and when they get here I don't want it cluttered up by you river rats—I'm giving you just twenty-four hours to gather up your stuff and get out."

If Big Bill had whipped Skip right there or thrown him in the river it probably would not have been as humiliating for this so-called mining promoter.

Instead, Bill simply laughed at him and dared Skip to do anything about it.

"I'll be right here when you and your mining men arrive," Bill told him. "And if I'm not here I'll be right over there at my camp. As for right now, you just get the hell outa here before I wear out what's left of this poor old boot of mine on your tail end."

Angry and red faced, Skip strode away, hurling threats involving the sheriff and the law and other dire consequences, and it was not an hour later he arrived at our tenthouse where I was chopping wood.

I didn't see Skip until he hollered at me.

"Hey, you—you're another one that better be packing up and getting out of here, because tomorrow I'm gonna be back with the sheriff and a posse and there's going to be a lot of shacks a-burning and a lot of you damned snipers headed for jail."

Startled, I straightened up and turned to see Skip bearing down on me, his face livid and contorted with rage.

I guess it was the ax I was still holding in my hands that stopped him short of violence, for he suddenly came to an abrupt halt but kept shouting threats at me.

"Mister," I told him, "I got just as much right here as you have, and you nor no other damn fool is gonna come shouting and threatening me."

I was mad clear through—so angry I was shaking, and if Dot hadn't heard the shouting and come to the tenthouse door I don't know what might have happened—maybe I would have taken after him with the ax.

"You get off this ground and you get off fast, and if I so much as catch you around here even looking like you might have a match in your hand you better damn well have more than a posse with you."

Dot came running out and put a stop to things, and Skip, now cursing loudly while Ladybug added to the general confusion with her barking, strode away, up the river trail.

It was not the last time I ever saw Skip, but it was the last time I saw him alive.

I sat down on the woodpile to try and regain my composure and, with shaking hands, rolled a cigarette.

Dot was scared. "Do you think he'll come back? Do you think maybe he means it about a posse or about trying to burn us out?"

"Hell no, he doesn't mean it—he's just a damn fool and he's drunk. He just wants to show us poor bastards here on the river what a big guy he is—he can go to hell."

I finished the cigarette, stomped it out with my heel, and went back to splitting wood. Maybe an hour had passed when I heard the dog begin barking, and then Dot screamed.

"Jess . . . Jess . . . Oh, my God . . . Jess, come quick!"

I dropped the ax, started on a dead run for the tenthouse and then I saw him—old Jack Murray, half-staggering, half-crawling, was at the edge at the clearing, his face a gaping mask of blood.

Poor Jack had been beaten or clubbed. As I grabbed to steady and half-carry him to the tenthouse I could see his jaw was broken and jagged stubs of teeth showed against his lacerated lips. His face and head were cut in a dozen places, his clothes were saturated with blood.

The old man was only half coherent and with his broken jaw he could hardly talk.

"Quick, Dot, get a towel and something we can use for bandages. We got to get him to a doctor, fast."

"Doctor . . . don't need no doctor. Get the sheriff—gonna need the sheriff, Jess—'cause I just shot a man."

I didn't have to ask who had been shot.

We loaded the poor, injured old man into the Chevvy and started for town, and a bit at a time, Jack told us what had happened.

He was cooking supper when he heard footsteps on his cabin porch and he turned around just in time to get hit squarely in the face with something—a chunk of wood, he thought.

"Never had a chance," he mumbled through broken lips. "Never had a chance—he knocked me down. I started to get up and he knocked me down again, started kicking me in the head."

Somehow, the old man had gotten his hands on his rifle, swung it up and fired.

We took Jack to the hospital and called the sheriff's office from there.

The sheriff met us, and while they attempted to patch up and wire Jack's broken jaw, I accompanied the sheriff, his deputy, and a couple of other men to the scene of the shooting.

The havoc wrought on human flesh by the full, one-ounce soft lead slug of a 45-70 rifle fired at point blank range is neither pretty nor simple to describe. The bullet had caught Skip squarely on the point of the chin and ranged upward, expanding as it hit bone.

The body was lying face downward in the middle of the blood-spattered cabin floor, and we identified it by the clothing in which it was clad, for there was no face left with which to make any other identification.

Jack Murray was arrested and six weeks later stood trial on a charge of manslaughter. When he testified from the witness stand he spoke with wires still holding his shattered jaw.

The jury deliberated little more than an hour before returning a verdict of "Not guilty."

CHAPTER VI

SLUG GULCH

AUGUST ARRIVED AND THE HEAT AT MIDDAY HUNG LIKE A PALL OVER the parched, brown foothills. No rain had fallen since April and each day the water level of the Agua Fria dropped perceptibly.

Stretches of the stream already were virtually dry. Fish and frogs had congregated in the few deeper pools fed by underground springs, and hardly a week went by that we did not see smoke billowing up on the horizon from some distant forest fire.

The dropping water level posed new problems for Dot and me in our mining operations. No longer could we simply set up our sluice box and shovel gravel into it.

Now, lack of water often forced us to carry the gravel in buckets or move it several yards by wheelbarrow from digging spot to sluice box. It slowed our mining operation, was considerably harder work, and sharply reduced the amount of gold we took home each day.

In fact, our gold recovery dropped from an average of two dollars and fifty cents or three dollars per day to little more than a dollar, and I knew that conditions would get no better until late October or November when fall rains would once again raise the stream level.

At different times and places I had often observed snipers

using a small pump powered by a one-cylinder gasoline engine which pushed water through a hose to their sluice boxes set up several yards from the edge of the stream.

This method was perfect for working high ground or gravel bars set back a distance from the water. It did away with the back-breaking work of carrying gravel, and it also eliminated the dip bucket used to wash gravel through the box.

Only the cost of such equipment had kept Dot and me from acquiring it long ago, for I was sure a good pump and engine with necessary length of hose would amount to at least a hundred dollars.

But one evening, after a day of endless trips over rough, broken bedrock carrying heavy buckets of gravel in which our total take amounted to a dollar fifteen, we made the decision. A pump and engine we were going to have, even if it meant digging deep into our meager resources.

Merced, some fifty miles away, was the town where we could make the purchase. Next morning, long before sunrise, I dug up the "poke," took out what I thought would cover the cost of the outfit (thanks to the rattlesnake who made this possible) and by sunup the old Chevvy was rattling along toward Mariposa and Highway 49.

We stopped in Mariposa to cash the gold dust just as the general store was opening. I didn't think a city-bred clerk in some hardware department would be particularly anxious to part with a pump and engine for a handful of yellow dust that some old codger told him was gold.

It had been so long since we had been to a large town that Merced on that hot summer day seemed like a teeming metropolis. The big Montgomery Ward store seemed like the busiest place in the world.

Dot had not worn high heels and a dress for so long that she said she felt everyone was staring at her.

But the store stocked exactly what we wanted, and a lot of

other things, too—like a new ax which I could have used very well—and new boots and clothes for both of us.

We left Montgomery Ward's with the pump and engine and an order for six twenty-foot lengths of light fire hose which would be shipped from San Francisco to Mariposa.

And to make things even better, after eating lunch in a coffee shop, there still was fifteen dollars left which prompted a shopping spree for groceries and a list of little seminecessities we had long put off buying.

Completely satisfied and played out, we arrived home at darkness to be greeted by Ladybug, who had spent the day on a leash in the shade of the tenthouse.

The hose for the pump arrived in due time, and meanwhile, I had scouted out a place some twenty yards from the stream bed that panned quite well and showed promise. I already had moved boulders to expose the thin layer of pay dirt and set up the sluice box in order that when the hose arrived there would be no lost motion in getting started.

As long as I live I will never forget that first day with the new pump and engine. With a steady stream of water flowing from the hose into the sluice box, I shoveled while Dot removed the large rocks from the box with a small sluice fork and broke up any particles held together by clay.

I worked steadily with the shovel, for now there was no need to stop and dip water to wash the gravel. The steady chugging of the little engine was music to my ears and the steady stream of water gushing into the sluice box was an added symphony.

There were no delays, and I was putting more gravel through the sluice box in a single morning than I ever had before.

Standing beside the box, Dot kept up a chatter like a split-tongued magpie, announcing with glee each glimpse of a color sliding down the box into the screen. But each time a tiny nugget showed up she would let out a screech, her hand would swoop down like a turkey hen gobbling a grain of corn, and into our clean-up bottle would go the piece of gold.

About noon I shut down the outfit to take time out for lunch. I was positive we already that morning had sluiced as much or more pay dirt than we had during the entire previous three days of mining.

A close look at the screen revealed a pretty fair concentration of fine gold, and I was well aware that with the upper half of the screen doubled we were only seeing part of what we had collected for our morning's work.

It was a short lunch hour, for both of us were anxious to get back to mining. The little engine chugged along steadily all afternoon until finally, about 4 P.M. I shut it off and we made our clean-up.

I knew we had moved a lot of gravel and that it was of fairly good value, but not until I saw that string of gold, wet and shining in the bottom of the gold pan, did I realize its actual volume. Back at camp I dumped the day's take onto the gold scales to find it weighed five pennyweights and one grain—exactly $7.56 at the going price of gold.

The next ten days were much the same, until we completely worked out that particular little spot. The pump and engine already had almost paid for itself and it had cut our labor in half.

Our last act at the spot where we had begun mining with the pump was to wash down the now exposed bedrock. Then I took a rock chisel, split out every seam and crevice, and cleaned the bedrock again.

The residue from the second cleaning contained a high percentage of clay, almost impossible to wash or work when in semiwet state. However, I gathered up every scrap and took it home to dry in the sun.

I planned to wait for rainy days, then pulverize it and pan it out. That clay was like money in the bank, and at the same time it would give me something to do when it was too stormy to work outside.

We located a second spot and worked it out quickly, but

each day the water level of the Agua Fria was dropping more rapidly. Long stretches of the creek bed were now dry, and the last day we worked at the second spot I was forced to build a little dam to create a pool large enough to pump from. I knew that within a matter of days the entire stream, except for the spring holes, would be dry.

Many of the snipers were moving out because of the lack of water with which to sluice, and most of those who remained were reduced to panning in the small seep holes that were left. It was a hell of a tough way to make a living.

The thing to do, as far as I was concerned, was to find another stream with enough water to run the pump. I settled on a fork of the Agua Fria which the old-timers had named Slug Gulch because of the heavy nuggets found there.

Slug Gulch was quite a hike from camp, but for a considerable distance it was spring fed and always had running water, even in the driest years.

Leaving Dot in camp, I walked the two miles over the next ridge from the Agua Fria and spent the day exploring Slug Gulch with shovel and gold pan. It was a narrow, twisting ravine, seldom more than ten feet wide from wall to wall. But there was gravel and crevices and, above all, a flow of running water with which to sluice.

The men who had mined Slug Gulch during gold rush days some eighty years before, had moved huge boulders and stacked them along the side of the ravine to form what was now a moss-covered wall.

I sampled here and there with the gold pan, raising a few colors. Then I hit a spot where it appeared that instead of sluicing it through their boxes, the original miners had shoveled the top foot or more of gravel overburden up onto the creekbank in order to get to the richer pay dirt near the bedrock.

Again I began sampling with the pan, and this time the prospects improved. From each pan of the gravel the old miners had shoveled onto the bank I recovered tiny bits of gold, but it was not the fine flour gold that was prevalent on the Agua Fria. There were not too many of them, but each piece was a tiny, pinhead-sized nugget. With luck, I figured, a man could make at least a few dollars a day.

The trip next day from camp to Slug Gulch with that eighty-pound pump on my back was not exactly any picnic. The ridge that separated Slug Gulch from the Agua Fria was steep and rocky and the slick dry grass and brush made the going no easier.

First the pump, then the engine, and finally the sluice box, hose, and tools. I made three trips that day, and although I don't suppose that in actual distance I had walked much more than ten miles, when I arrived in camp from the last hike over the ridge I felt more as if I had walked forty miles.

Although actually we were working less hours at mining because of the distance we had to travel to and from camp, our first days on Slug Gulch were profitable. Working the gravel those long-forgotten men had cast up on the creekbank brought us an average of about five dollars a day. Most of the gold continued to contain a coarseness we had not seen on the Agua Fria.

But after a few days the supply of gravel which had been thrown aside by the old-timers gave out. We were in the process of cleaning up the last of it when one day at noon I idly rolled several boulders from the rock wall stacked against the opposite side of the ravine. One large rock, weighing perhaps two hundred pounds, formed the bottom of the wall at that particular spot. Without too much effort, and really without too much definite purpose in mind, I used the shovel to pry it from the spot where it had been resting for nearly a century.

To my surprise, instead of smooth bedrock behind where this boulder lay, there was a strip of gravel about a foot wide and a foot deep. I grabbed the gold pan, scooped a shovelful of the sand and pebbles into it, and swirled it in the water.

Two minutes later I sat in amazement staring at a nugget the size of a large lima bean, surrounded by a scattering of smaller ones.

I tore down another section of the rock wall and, to my utter disbelief, there behind the sheltering rocks which had hidden it for so many years was the same strip of gravel.

We tore down the wall in several other places, and at each spot there was the strip of gravel which had either been overlooked or ignored by the old-timers. In all, the wall was nearly a hundred yards long, and the streak of gravel ran the full length of it.

The gravel was rich, for it was part of the original stream bed, and it contained nuggets that ranged in value from two dollars and fifty cents to as much as fifteen dollars. I estimated it would average about two dollars and fifty cents a foot, but it was anything but easy mining.

How those old miners had managed to lift and stack some of those boulders, I just don't know. Some of them, I'm sure, weighed as much as five hundred pounds, and few weighed less than fifty. I strained every muscle in my body moving them from their resting places to the other side of the creek. At least half of them I could not lift at all, but moved them with a crowbar, a few inches at a time.

Seldom did we manage to work more than seven or eight feet of wall in a day, and sometimes, when the boulders were really large, we worked less. But we worked it all; every inch of that gravel slid through our sluice box before we were through, and I cleaned the crevices until they were polished. We averaged just about fourteen dollars per day—by far the best ground we ever found in Mariposa County.

By now we were well into September and there was a definite hint of fall in the air those mornings as we climbed the ridge from camp to drop down to our workings in Slug Gulch.

Word of our good fortune got out, and unsuspectingly I almost triggered a gold rush. Without thinking, I took some of the nuggets from Slug Gulch into town and cashed them at the general store.

The store owner, accustomed to seeing only fine gold in which a small pea-sized nugget was more or less unusual, was all eyes and questions when I dumped some five ounces of gold containing several nuggets of more than ten dollars each, onto his gold scales.

Realizing what I had started, I tried to pass it off casually. "Hit a little sweet spot," I said. "A crevice the old-timers overlooked, I guess." But neither the store owner nor several loafers standing nearby who had suddenly become interested onlookers were completely satisfied with my explanation. It was no secret that Dot and I had recently abandoned the Agua Fria and moved our operations to Slug Gulch.

The story of our strike was all over town within a couple of hours, and the story apparently had grown with the telling. Next day we had several visitors. In fact, within the week, several of the snipers on the Agua Fria also had moved their mining operations to Slug Gulch.

Luckily by the time that I did cash in the first of the Slug Gulch gold we had pretty well cleaned up all of the rock wall. There was only about another twenty-five or thirty yards left to work, but none of the others could quite summon up the audacity to move right beside us.

It was November by the time we finished mining out the rich spot on Slug Gulch, and already there had been a couple of good, solid, fall rains. The Agua Fria, dry a month ago, was now flowing again. Dot and I now had to pick our way from rock to rock when we crossed it on our way to Slug Gulch.

Several days of sniping along other sections of Slug Gulch revealed little to attract us. Most of the stream was hard bedrock which had been worked from rim to rim. There were few gravel bars, and most of them turned out to be of low value. Most of the men who had followed us over there after our rich strike had already returned to the Agua Fria.

We found one little spot, a small gravel bar a few hundred yards downstream from the rock wall. Here, for a short time, we averaged about a dollar seventy-five for a day's work, but this, too, gave out.

Slug Gulch had been good to us. Our three months' work had brought us $792, but both of us felt the time had come to call it quits there and hunt for a place on the Agua Fria to resume mining.

We also made another decision, and agreed that another trip to Merced was in order.

My old leather boots were in shreds, the rubber boots I wore when mining had holes in both soles. The elbows were out of my old jacket, and my best pair of Levi's had patches holding on the patches. Dot was almost in as bad a shape as far as work or camp clothes were concerned, and with winter coming, new and warmer clothing was a necessity.

We spent more than sixty dollars in Merced on clothes and other necessities. A new green and white plaid mackinaw and leather boots for me. Levi's and a couple of good work shirts and a pair of brand-new hip boots for mining. Dot also splurged —or at least she said she did—and bought new clothes from underwear on out. Her last purchase was a pair of navy blue wool blankets. "We'll sleep warm this winter," she said.

We bought a new ax, a Coleman lantern, and just as we were about to leave the store, Dot rushed back to the shoe department and bought herself a pair of woolly, sheepskin-lined slippers for those cold winter mornings.

The weather suddenly turned wet and for several days I sniped up and down the Agua Fria in drizzling rain. Dot and Ladybug stayed in camp while I prospected for another place to start mining, for there was little reason for them to be miserable, too.

I finally located a little piece of high bar that produced a fair bit of color, and upon returning home that day at noon I decided to walk back over to Slug Gulch and get the pump and engine we had left there.

By midafternoon I returned with the pump, and then, although Dot suggested I wait until next morning to make another trip over the ridge for the gasoline engine, I decided to bring it home that day. As I made my way up the slope toward Slug Gulch, it seemed to be raining harder, and by the time I got there and started back, I knew damned well the rain had increased.

I was soaked to the skin, and upon reaching Agua Fria on the return trip with the engine, the rain had turned into a downpour. The water in the creek had risen at least three inches in the two hours it had taken me to walk to Slug Gulch and back.

I splashed across the creek, now almost knee deep, and arrived at the tenthouse dripping and exhausted. In the gathering darkness I covered pump and engine with a canvas and with the rain falling in blinding sheets, ran for the warm comfort of our shelter.

As we ate supper the rain pelted the tenthouse with increasing fury, and a howling, blustery wind was building up, driving each droplet like a piece of buckshot.

Several times during the night the storm awakened me as sheets of water slammed against our canvas roof and sharp puffs of wind shook the entire structure.

It still was raining next morning, a steady downpour that had not let up all night, and the rain continued into the day. The river was more than a foot higher than it had been the night before, and had turned a dirty chocolate brown. Small logs and pieces of driftwood were already racing down in the swirling current.

After breakfast I put on a rain slicker and my new hip boots with the intention of trying to drive the old Chevvy to the top of the hill above the camp. I knew that once the narrow trace of a road that led from our campsite to the top of the ridge got muddy the car might be stranded at camp indefinitely.

Braving the rain, I jacked up the hind wheels of the car and installed tire chains, then after letting the engine warm up I gave the hill a try. At first it wasn't bad because I had plenty of momentum, and during the initial hundred yards or so the old Chevvy ground on up the hill without slipping or spinning a wheel. The second hundred yards was not so good, for now I had lost speed and I hit a slick spot which started the old car wallowing from side to side. Then the wheels started spinning.

But I made it a distance farther, sloughing and skidding up the hill, with engine racing. Both rear wheels now were slipping and spinning more than they were making headway.

I might have made it clear to the top except that just before the road reached the crest of the ridge there was an especially steep, little pitch, and there I stalled.

I tried that last little hump a couple more times, but each time the car stalled out and I ended up backing down the hill to a fairly level spot at the foot of the steep grade.

Finally, realizing I was not going to make it to the top, and that all my efforts were only chewing up the road and making it more slippery, I gave up. I draped a small piece of canvas over the hood and radiator of the car, weighted them down with rocks, and started back for camp in the pouring rain.

After changing into dry clothes, I spent the remainder of the day in the tent pulverizing and panning the dried clay we had collected from cracks in the bedrock, while the rain continued to come down. Only once did I venture out, and that was to walk down and drive a stake into the gravel at the water's edge in order to measure the rise of the river.

Darkness came and we ate dinner while the storm still raged outside. Not once during the day had the rain lessened. The stake I had driven into the ground at the edge of the water was now several feet out into the stream and the water had raised at least two feet on it. I estimated that the river now had risen three feet since the start of the storm.

It was raining steadily when we went to bed and still raining the next morning. I looked out the window to see how much the water had risen on my measuring stick, but it was gone, apparently knocked down by floating driftwood or the large logs that were now cluttering the stream.

The Agua Fria was a raging torrent, and I estimated it now had risen at least four feet.

We were eating breakfast when suddenly I heard heavy boots stomping on our doorstep and someone was pounding on the door.

Bill McCarty stumbled in out of the storm, his clothes hanging on him like wet rags. He was breathing hard from having traveled fast, and there was an air of urgency in his manner.

"Jess, we need your help . . . old Jack—Jack Murray—is down at my cabin hurt real bad! He's gotta busted leg and I think maybe he's comin' down with pneumonia. He was movin' his sluice box and tools up outa the way of the high water some time yesterday when he slipped and fell. Spent most of the night crawling and dragging himself down to my camp, and I found him at daylight this morning when I went out to get wood.

"He's real bad," Bill went on. "Real sick and half out of his head. If we don't get him into town and into the hospital, he's gonna die!"

There was no time to waste and I knew it. Without even finishing breakfast, I climbed into my rain clothes and started down the narrow, slippery river trail toward Bill's camp.

We arrived half an hour later and I found that Bill certainly had not exaggerated. Jack's leg was fractured between his knee and hip, and he was delirious with pain and exhaustion.

Both Bill and I knew it would be too big a job for just the two of us to try to carry Jack out by ourselves on an improvised stretcher. The only thing to do was to get more help. I started off downstream again to find Big Tom and Red Whiskers while Bill stayed with old Jack and fashioned a stretcher.

Big Tom and Red Whiskers, both giants of men, would be of immeasurable help, and luckily, both were in their camps staying out of the rain.

An hour later I was back with the two men. Bill had made a stretcher of two poles and a couple of blankets and we were ready to travel with our injured man.

The trip back up that wet, slippery canyon trail was a nightmare. I don't think old Jack weighed much more than one hundred and sixty pounds, but it was all dead weight, and each step we took found our feet sliding on mud and wet treacherous rocks. It was only the bull strength of Big Tom and that giant Finlander that got us through some of those steep rocky places on the trail, but nevertheless, we traveled fast. Sweat mixed with rain ran down our faces and got into our eyes.

Well before noon we arrived at Dot's and my camp, and we paused only long enough to replace the wet blankets around old Jack with dry ones. Then we started up the hill to where the Chevvy had stalled the day before on the steep, slick road.

If I could possibly make it the rest of the way up the hill in the car, things would be all right, we would have Jack in the hospital in another hour or so. But, if the hill was just too slick to make it, then it would mean carrying our patient most of the day through driving rain, and I wasn't sure any of us would make it.

We arrived at the car and, good old work horse that it was, it started. We loaded Jack into the vehicle with his temporarily splinted leg lying as straight as possible, then with the three men pushing, I started up the last steep part of the hill.

That extra little push was what was needed. The Chevvy spun and gasped and coughed, and it threw mud by the bucketful on the men pushing it, but with just a single try we made it to the top of the hill.

Mud-spattered, soaking wet, looking like refugees from a hog pen, we carried Jack on the homemade stretcher into the old frame building that served as the hospital.

It was late that night, and the rain had slackened but little when we arrived back at our tenthouse on the Agua Fria. We were still soaked and wet and dirty, but Dot had a roaring fire going in the little stove and a big pot of venison stew waiting for us.

Bill and Tom and Red Whiskers crowded around the table with us, filled their plates and ate as the warm fire sent clouds of steam wafting upward from their rain-soaked clothes. By the time they were ready to leave the rain had become a drizzle.

As for old Jack, he was a tough old buzzard. A week later he was back stomping around his camp with a crutch and a cast on his leg. Of course, he could not mine, and in those days welfare was just about unheard of. We all pitched together and saw that he had enough to eat and get by on until he was able to go back to mining again.

CHAPTER VII

PORCUPINES ARE NOT MY FAVORITE ANIMALS

PORCUPINES ARE NOT MY FAVORITE ANIMALS.

A deer in the wild is a thing of beauty and, around a camp, squirrels and chipmunks soon become playful, entertaining pets. Even bear, although sometimes destructive as tornados when they venture into an unattended camp or cabin, are generally no more than harmless clowns. I can even adopt a live and let live attitude toward skunks.

But old Porky, slow-witted, shuffling oaf that he is, will chew up your ax handle, polish off your work gloves for dessert, then fill your dog's nose full of quills when the dog comes out to chase him away.

Porky is too stupid to be afraid of anything and, when cornered, simply rolls himself into a ball and lashes out with his pin-cushion tail at anything which comes within reach. He is essentially a bark eater but he loves salt and will go to any lengths to get it. In their quest for anything with even a saline taint, porcupines will amble into a camp and chew the handle right off your frying pan.

Just about every place I've ever mined or camped seems to have had more than its share of porcupines, and the Agua Fria was no exception.

We had been there only a couple of weeks when, arriving at my sluice box one morning, I was made painfully aware that our area had its porcupine population. During the night a porky had visited my mining spot and gnawed half my shovel handle away to get the salt worked into it from the perspiration of my hands.

A few days later, Dot and I returned home from the river to find a huge, old porky contentedly engaged in chewing up the seat of our one-holer.

Like most of the foothill country along the Mother Lode, the Agua Fria, where we were sniping, was good game country.

Deer, mostly does and fawns, wandered right into camp. During our first spring and summer there Dot fought a constant and sometimes losing battle with them and with their raccoon and ground squirrel allies for possession of the vegetable garden she planted.

We looked upon the area around our camp as sort of an animal sanctuary. Although I hunted cottontails, gray squirrels, and quail with the little .410 shotgun to supplement our food supply, I never hunted or shot a bird or animal close to camp.

The deer and Dorothy continued to contest each other for the produce from her garden plot. They cropped the tomato vines, trimmed the peas and string beans, and most of the other vegetables. However, they pointedly ignored and refused even to nibble on her stand of corn, which, in the river loam, began to put on astounding height. The stalks were heavy with big, sweet-kerneled ears and Dot was counting the days until the first of them would be harvestable, when near disaster struck.

Just at dawn one morning Ladybug awakened us by whining and scratching at the tenthouse door. Half awake, I stumbled out of bed and opened it for her. She darted out and, a moment later, a frenzy of barking and growling burst forth from the garden patch.

I ran outside just in time to see an old mama raccoon, followed by her half-grown brood, hightailing it from the corn patch with Ladybug in irate pursuit.

The corn itself was a shambles of bent and broken stalks. Many of the almost ripened ears had been ruined by the family of coons which had moved from one to another taking only a single bite or two from each ear.

Dot joined me, and when she observed the damage she sat down right there in the middle of the corn patch and cried.

We knew unless something was done promptly that between the deer and the raccoons, and ground squirrels who ate our squash and melons, we would have no garden.

The deer had become so bold and accustomed to Ladybug that when she tried to chase them away they would run from her only a short distance, then turn around and chase her back again.

We solved the problem and saved our vegetable crop by moving our bed out of the tenthouse into the garden to keep the amimals out of it at night. It really wasn't a bad arrangement, since it was summer and sleeping out-of-doors was enjoyable. The animals, at least the deer and raccoons, stopped eating our garden and the mosquitoes only ate us a little bit.

It was during this period we were mining a small gravel bar nearly a mile upstream from camp. We had moved our operation there because most of the better mining spots closer to camp had been pretty well worked out, and this particular tree-shaded section of the stream provided relief from the hot summer sun while we were working.

It was not a particularly rich spot, the gold was fine and we were averaging between a dollar and a half and two dollars per day with shovel, crevicing tools, and dip box. But it was better than most prospectors along the river were doing—and it was eating money, anyway.

Shortly after noon one day, I hit a deep crevice, and the tightly packed gravel in it looked more promising than usual.

I scooped out several shovels full, dumped them into the sluice box and began washing the gravel, picking out the larger rocks by hand. As the amount of gravel diminished to pebbles and fine sand, I suddenly saw a gleam of yellow appear on the screen in the bottom of the box. I fished it out with my fingers, a smooth, partially flattened, buckshot-sized nugget.

Still holding the wet, glistening piece of gold, I motioned to Dot, who had been scraping bedrock a few feet away from me.

"Look here, kid, here's a nice little chunk to add to your collection—"

But suddenly, I realized Dot was no longer kneeling there on the bedrock, nor was she looking at the nugget I had found.

Instead, she was standing, staring intently into the woods behind us.

"Jess . . . look there . . . right on that rock—that big rock by the tree—"

She spoke in a frightened stage whisper, her voice filled with apprehension.

I swung around, and there, some fifty yards up the hill from the creek, sprawled out on a big, flat-topped boulder like a lazy, oversized tomcat, was a mountain lion.

He lay there, watching us casually, a sleek, tawny shadow, perfectly motionless except for an occasional twitch of the tip of his tail.

It was the first and only mountain lion either of us had ever seen. One moment he was there, and the next moment he was gone, melted into the brush and shadows of the hillside.

Dot stood there, still staring at the rock where the lion had been, looking as if she was ready to run.

"Will he come back? . . . Will he attack us?" she asked.

"No, he won't come back, and he isn't about to attack anybody. Mountain lions don't attack people. He was just simply curious, and as soon as he realized we had seen him, he left."

But I don't think I did a very good job of convincing my wife of the harmlessness of mountain lions. About all she did the rest of the afternoon was try to watch in two directions at once, and I don't think at any time she got more than three steps away from me.

Usually about midafternoon, Dot took off from our diggings

to go back to camp so she could water the garden and get supper started. But this particular afternoon she was quite content to stay until I finished work, and then on the trail home she made me walk behind her. Dot was not going to have any mountain lion sneak up and bite her when she wasn't looking.

Actually, in all the years we spent in the mountains only once was I placed in a spot with a wild animal where I actually felt real apprehension or that my safety was in jeopardy.

That incident, however, occurred on the Yuba River shortly after we had moved our sniping operations to Sierra County. We were living in a cabin at the time, and in those days Sierra County was a considerably more primitive country than the Agua Fria.

Dot had caught a dozen trout during the afternoon and we put them in the meat safe with plans to fry them for breakfast.

Sometime during the early morning hours Dot poked me awake with her elbow.

There was a rattling and banging outside where the meat safe was located and Ladybug began barking furiously.

"Jess . . . Jess! Wake up, there's something out there trying to get those trout."

"Those damned raccoons," I said as I jumped out of bed, grabbed a flashlight and the .410, and dashed outside barefooted and in my BVD's. Had I stopped to think, I might have taken a different course of action, for I would have noted that although Ladybug still was barking angrily at the door, she made no effort to dash outside when I opened it.

I rounded the corner of the cabin and came face to face with a large black bear who was standing on his hind legs holding a fish in his mouth. At the range of about four feet, I skidded to a halt, the weak beam of the flashlight centered on the bear's ugly jowls.

I don't think he was really a big bear, but from where I stood he appeared to have the stature of an Alaskan Kodiak. He blinked his beady little eyes, uttered what sounded to me to be a menacing snarl, and instead of running as most bears always do, he chomped down on the fish and stood his ground. It was I who was doing the backing up, and the little shotgun loaded with No. 6 shot that I was holding in my hand seemed to be growing smaller all the time. Against that bear it would have had about the same effectiveness as a water pistol.

I reached the corner of the cabin, made a jump for the door and slammed it behind me. I guess it was the noise of the slamming door that did it, for I heard another crash and then the thud of the bear's feet as he took off for the brush.

A bit later, after things had quieted down and we were pretty sure the bear had really departed, we went back out to survey the damage. The meat safe was a wreck and every one of the fish was gone.

"That darned old bear," said Dot. "He's wrecked the meat safe and all those lovely fish are gone!"

"Yes," I replied, "but you've still got your lovely husband, and for a while I thought you might be needing a replacement for him, too."

That little incident did it. Next morning I drove into town and bought a good secondhand 30-30 Winchester. We never had another bear in camp as long as we were there.

Few of the snipers along the Agua Fria had dogs or cats. Mostly, they couldn't afford to feed the dogs, and the cats had to pretty much forage for themselves until sooner or later they usually got bushwhacked by a coyote or bobcat.

But that is not to say that many of them did not have pets. Some made friends with ground squirrels which became tame enough to eat from their hands. Others made a habit of feeding birds bread crumbs and their few table scraps until they became virtually domesticated.

Mice are always a problem around a permanent camp, and there is no better mouser than a skunk. Several of the miners along the Agua Fria (Big Tom was one of them) deliberately cultivated the friendship of a family of skunks who took up residence under a pile of logs a few yards from his cabin. He fed them his table scraps and in return they kept his camp free of mice.

The skunks became so friendly he could approach within a couple of feet of them. They never once released their powerful scent around his camp, and in the evenings, the young ones often played much as kittens do, around the front yard of his cabin.

The ring-tailed cat or cacomistle, as the Spanish called it, is a golden colored little animal about the size of a small house cat with a black ringed tail nearly as long as his body.

There are few of them in the foothills, but they domesticate easily, and are one of the few wild animals which truly become nice pets. A miner we knew had one of them which became so tame it would come into his tenthouse and, in his absence, sleep on his bed. It was one of the prettiest, cleanest, and most interesting animals I have ever seen. It also was a master mouse catcher and he had few problems from the destructive little rodents after his ring-tailed cat settled there.

Several snipers at one time or another caught baby raccoons and tried to raise them as pets. They tamed down pretty well, and were always a source of humor with their clever antics, but they never really became too tame, and they would steal anything that wasn't nailed down.

As for our own experiences with skunks, we had numerous ones. Skunks were plentiful in our foothill country and they had no qualms whatsoever about coming into camp at dusk to investigate Ladybug's food dish on the chance she might have left a morsel or two.

The first time this happened, Ladybug saw the skunk before we did and dashed out to irately defend her half-eaten dinner. That was her first and only mistake with skunks, and our camp could easily be located by the smell alone for several days thereafter.

As for Ladybug, Dot bathed her with at least three different kinds of soap, saturated her with vinegar, and finally ended up pouring most of a bottle of perfume over her in an effort to rid her of the skunk smell. Nevertheless, for a month after her encounter Ladybug still smelled of skunk every time she got wet.

One particular afternoon as I neared camp about 4:30 P.M., I noticed that no plume of smoke was issuing from the tenthouse chimney. Then, I spotted Dot seated on a rock some fifty yards in front of the camp.

Even before I could speak, Dot stood up and began waving at me to halt.

"Don't go near the tenthouse," she called. "The place is full of skunks!"

Somehow the screen door had come open during the day and an old mother skunk and her youngsters had wandered in. The attraction was a sack of dry dog food which Dot always kept on the floor near the stove. We were forced to sit in the yard for an hour while the skunks stuffed themselves on dog food. Finally, completely unconcerned, the skunk with her half-grown babies, wandered back outside and off to the woods again, their bellies fairly bulging.

From that day on, we made sure the screen door was latched when we left to go mining in the mornings.

Certainly, the animals along the Agua Fria—with the possible exception of the procupines—did us and the other snipers no harm, and they were an ever-present source of interest and entertainment.

But the porcupines we could have done without.

One morning just as we were preparing to leave for work, a prospector who had recently set up camp a half mile downriver from us, arrived to ask for help.

This fellow—I can't recollect his name—owned a large Airedale dog, and it had tangled with a procupine. He needed help to extract the quills.

When we arrived at this fellow's camp where he had the dog tied to a tree, the poor animal was frantic with pain. Its face was a solid pincushion of quills. They were embedded in his nose, lips, and tongue. Apparently, the dog had been slapped the first time with the porcupine's tail, then had tried to bite it and had gotten the quills in his mouth.

Normally a quite gentle animal, the dog fought us if we tried to even touch his face. We finally ended up hog-tying him, and it required all of his owner's strength and mine to hold the squirming, writhing beast down while Dot extracted the deeply embedded quills with a pair of pliers. A half hour later, when she had finished, she had a total of fifty-three quills.

From that day on, I declared war on porcupines, and even today I will go out of my way to shoot one, although I am not a man who takes enjoyment in killing anything.

I have found cattle starving because they had been hit in the face by a procupine's tail and could not feed, and I once found a dead fawn, its face covered with quills.

Maybe the porcupine has a place in the ecology of the wild, but I don't know where it is. He will decimate a whole grove of young evergreens by stripping the bark off of them.

As for that old tale that porkies should be protected because they are the only animal in the wild that a lost, unarmed man can run down and kill with a club, that might be true.

But a lost man could do a lot of wandering before he ever found one, and after he did find one and kill it, he would sure need a helluva sharp knife to get its hide off before it would do him much good. I've never heard of a lost man yet who saved himself by eating a porcupine.

CHAPTER VIII

BACON AND BEANS

TABLE FARE OF THE MAN WHO MINED FOR A LIVING DURING THE 1930s, generally making little more than a dollar a day, didn't exactly rival that of the Waldorf.

Often he was ten miles from the nearest store, reached only by walking steep, winding roads or trails thick with dust in summer and slick with mud in winter. Seldom did he own an automobile, and trips to town were made only when absolutely necessary. Furthermore, when he got there his pocketbook dictated that his hard-earned dollars go for items other than frills or exotic foods.

Bacon and beans were pretty much the average sniper's menu during those Depression days, and such things as fresh beef or pork seldom graced his table. In fact, even fresh vegetables were seldom a part of his regular diet.

Potatoes, flour, bacon, beans, canned milk, and coffee were his staples. The meat he ate was what fell to his gun, and generally he would not take time to plant a garden. Why some of those men we knew who existed on that kind of diet did not come down with scurvy is something I have never been able to figure out. I guess they were tough.

Most of those prospectors ate terrible meals because they were terrible cooks, and secondly, a man who labors all day on the end of a pick and shovel doesn't feel much like returning to camp at night to spend another couple hours preparing some fancy dish. They ate what was fastest and easiest to prepare, with a frying pan as their principal culinary instrument. I've eaten meals thrown together by some of those prospectors that would have given a coyote colic.

Yet, the foothill country was not inhospitable, and although dollars were short, a person who wanted to make the effort could add considerable variation to his diet from the country itself.

For meat there was a variety of game that ranged from quail and wild pigeons to cottontails, gray squirrel, deer, and in the higher country, a few bear. There were trout for the catching, and depending upon a man's knowledge of the out-of-doors, there was a variety of wild fruits, nuts, and various greens and herbs all for the finding.

With the fall rains the foothills turned green, and suddenly, overnight, the first crop of pink-gilled field mushrooms appeared on the warmer slopes and swales.

We had been camped on the Agua Fria only a few weeks when the first fall rain hit. A few days later, while returning home from sluicing one afternoon, we crossed a grassy swale and I spotted the white caps of mushrooms among the blades of newly sprouted green grass.

I began picking them, and having nothing else to put them in, I filled my hat. Dot stood by watching, completely aghast that I was gathering what she was sure was going to turn out to be deadly toadstools.

"How do you know those are mushrooms—that they aren't poisonous?" she asked. But I continued to pick all I could find while she stood there, spouting prophesies of doom. Upon reaching camp, I carefully peeled and cleaned them.

Dot would have nothing to do with mushrooms, in fact she would not even cook them, and I had to fry them in butter myself.

"People are not going to be able to say that I contributed to my own widowhood," she told me.

I used the mushrooms to garnish my plate of rabbit stew, and all evening long Dot kept watching me, waiting for me to keel over, clutch my stomach and begin kicking in mortal agony. In fact, when I didn't, I think she was a little disappointed.

I gathered mushrooms at every opportunity, and finally, I enticed her to taste them, but I'm sure the snake didn't have as much trouble talking Eve into taking that first bite out of the apple.

Lo and behold, Dot found that mushrooms were good. From that time on she helped me gather them after carefully learning the difference between mushrooms and toadstools. In fact, whenever we found more than we could use at one time we picked them anyway, strung the excess on a string and hung them between the rafters over the stove to dry. Many a delicious stew we had after that during the dead of winter was seasoned with dried mushrooms.

Spring came, and although we always bought vegetables on our weekly visits to town, we still were hungry for fresh greens. I remembered something my dad had taught me many years ago when we went on one of our first hikes. In shaded spots on the edge of oak thickets grew a plant called miner's lettuce, which appeared early each spring. Its thin green stems with circular leaf growing around them was unmistakable, and our country along the Agua Fria abounded with the plants. Along with fresh green watercress the miner's lettuce provided salads.

Another wild spring vegetable that most of the prospectors simply passed up was fiddleheads.

Fiddleheads are nothing more than new green shoots of the huge sword ferns that grow along creeks and streams of the mountains and foothills in the Mother Lode. They derive their name from their shape—like that of the head of tiny violins. They are cooked and eaten and taste much like asparagus.

The first berries of summer to ripen are elderberries. Their cream-colored blossoms dot the hillsides in late April and early

May, and by mid-June the first of them, huge, clusters of berries as big as dinner plates, are ripe.

Each berry is about the size of a large BB-shot, full of tart purple juice. They are excellent for pie, but they make even better jelly, and we picked buckets full which Dot boiled down for jelly that served us during winter.

Wild raspberries were not plentiful, but now and then we happened onto a patch of them—blackcaps, the natives called them—and they are among the tastiest of all the wild berries.

If we could find enough, Dot would use them for pie, but usually a whole berry patch netted little more than a handful, for they are not prolific producers, and the birds also liked the ripe raspberries as well as we did. Unless there was a large supply we usually ate them as we picked them, stuffing them into our mouths, and their rich juice turned our lips and fingers red.

Then, along would come July, and the big, thumb-sized wild blackberries would begin ripening. Although we called them wild blackberries, they actually are blackberries gone wild, for they are not really native to California. Early settlers brought the blackberries from the East, and gradually they have spread to almost every stream and creek along the Mother Lode.

The best blackberries grow near water, producing large, sweet fruit that we used for pie and for jelly and jam. The only trouble with gathering blackberries is that they are full of murderous, sharp thorns, and the thick clusters of bushes make wonderful hiding places for rattlesnakes.

We averaged about one rattlesnake for each blackberry gathering trip, and I would get so jumpy from worrying about snakes I would make a ten-foot standing broadjump every time a bird fluttered in the berry bushes in front of me.

Nomads never plant orchards, but the early settlers who came to the foothills in the 1800s came to stay. They hacked and grubbed out clearings where there were springs, built their homes from logs or rough-sawed lumber, and planted orchards—apples, pears, grapes, plums, and black walnut trees.

The settlers and their houses were gone, and brush once again choked the clearings, but the old orchards, struggling against encroachment of the forest were still there, each year bearing their crops of fruit for birds and squirrels and deer or occasional wandering bruin.

We found many of these old orchards, sometimes just an apple tree or two remaining, others with whole groves of trees, untended for half-a-century. But in the fall the apples were sweet, the plums made wonderful jam, and the walnuts, when we could beat the squirrels to them, provided the material for nut bread and added dressing to cake frostings.

The country and its produce helped us live well because we took the time and effort to use what it provided.

One fall afternoon when out hunting with Bill McCarty's rifle I paused to take a short breathing spell after climbing a steep slope, and leaned against a dead, weather-whitened snag of an oak tree. Suddenly a honeybee zoomed past my ear, and seconds later another one, and then another buzzed past me. I jumped back to find I had been leaning almost against a knot-hole in the tree trunk from which was emerging a steady stream of bees.

Higher in the tree was a second hole from which flew an even heavier string of bees.

That evening when I returned the rifle and a haunch of fresh venison to Bill, I told him about my bee tree discovery. Bill was far more enthused about the prospects of fresh wild honey than he was about the deer meat, and immediately began making plans to rob the tree. I knew virtually nothing about handling bees, but Bill, who said he had worked around them, began laying plans and listing equipment we would need.

Next afternoon, loaded down with buckets, ax, cross-cut saw, rags, and chunks of mosquito netting to put around our heads, we started off up the ridge toward the dead oak beehive. Dot accompanied us, but as we drew near the tree my wife chose to remain a spectator at least until she saw how the bees were going to react to invasion of their privacy.

Once on the scene, Bill took command of the operation, and his first act was to cut a thin, fishing rod-sized pole about ten feet long. To the end of the pole he attached the rags with a piece of bailing wire, and then set them afire. Smoke, rank and acrid, billowed up from the smoldering rags, and meanwhile, the bees continued traveling in and out of the two holes in the dead oak, completely ignoring our activities.

While Bill had been fixing the rags, I had carefully tied the piece of mosquito netting around my head. My hatbrim held the netting away from my face, and I tied the ends of it around my neck to keep bees from getting under it.

With smoke pouring heavily from the rags, Bill, ignoring the mosquito netting, hoisted the stick until the burning rags were only inches from the main entrance at the hive some ten feet above the ground.

Bees came pouring out, swirled around in an angry mass, and although only a few were partially stupefied by the smoke, the others made no attempt to attack Bill who was standing at the base of the tree.

Bill instructed me to light a second bunch of rags and get them burning at the mouth of the lower entrance to the hive. For twenty minutes our bundles of rags smoldered, and when the number of bees appeared to have slacked off, Bill announced it was time to begin the next operation.

With cross-cut saw we began the job of felling the tree which was some twenty inches in diameter. The whitened shell of the old tree was bone hard, but its center was soft and punky and easy cutting. Bees continued to swarm around us, buzzing angrily only inches from our faces, but not a single insect actually attempted to sting.

With a resounding crash the old oak snag hit the ground in a cloud of dust and shattered, rotten wood.

A cloud of bees burst into the air around the remains of their hive and I started to run, but Bill shouted for me not to move. "Just stand still—if you run they will catch the movement and really go after you!" I managed to stay there in one spot without moving a muscle while every inclination was to put as much distance as possible between me and that mass of bees.

But surprisingly, the insects did not attack us, and instead, began gathering around the cracked and broken tree trunk. Then we saw why. Chunks of comb-filled honey were strewn through the shattered upper portion of the old tree and the bees were eating it.

Without hesitation, Bill waded in among the bees and with the ax began prying the tree trunk apart. "Bring a bucket—quick—bring all the buckets!"

The whole interior of the tree trunk was hollow, and great layers of honeycomb now lay exposed. With bees crawling on his hands and arms Bill scooped up slabs of comb and dumped them into the buckets. Even I lost my fear in the excitement and began scooping up honey. We filled one bucket, then another, and then the third and fourth buckets, packing the honeycomb in as tightly as possible.

I looked up and there was Dot right in the middle of things with us, having an absolute ball. She ignored the bees that crawled on her hands and on her shirt and buzzed around her.

In ten minutes it was all over. We had at least ten gallons of mixed comb and honey in the buckets and had withdrawn from the scene, each holding a big chunk of comb from which we licked the rich clear honey. The bees still swarmed around the fallen tree eating remnants we had left.

"I feel like a mean old robber," commented Dot, "but I don't feel so mean that I can't enjoy this honey."

"Best stuff in the world when you put it on hotcakes," replied Bill.

I was just opening my mouth to add to the conversation when I felt something crawling inside the mosquito netting I had pulled partially away so I could eat honey. Without thinking

I reached up and swatted at it, and next instant a dagger pierced my earlobe.

I let out a yell that shook the pine trees, dropped the chunk of comb I was holding and tried to yank off the netting which was still partially tied around my neck. Offending bee, net, and my hat went flying while Bill and Dot went into convulsions of laughter.

Things finally settled down and we started for camp with our honey, tools, and one badly puffed up ear.

Next day we rendered the honey out of the comb by heating it and placed it in jars. In all, we divided more than five gallons of pure honey with Bill, and had so much that even after selling some of it in town, there was more than enough to last us all winter.

The people who lived along the river ate venison in season and out, but they wasted nothing, and certainly the game warden who patroled that area was aware of what was going on. For many of us, it was eat wild game or go hungry, and the warden knew it. He would spend days and weeks running down outsiders who spotlighted deer at night, or those who killed deer when they really did not need the meat.

But I don't know of a single prospector, living from hand to mouth, who occasionally killed a deer because he was hungry, who was arrested.

In fact, the warden often stopped at the store or post office and casually announced that he had heard "those damned snipers down on the river killing deer again" and he was going down next day to investigate.

He would arrive, check a few camps, and leave without finding a shred of evidence, for just as he had intended, word of his impending visit had preceded him.

Occasionally I killed a deer, using a borrowed rifle, and when I did, we shared the venison with whomever I borrowed the rifle from, and with other neighbors along the river. By the same token, they shared venison with us when they made a kill.

But generally I stuck to small game—quail, cottontail rabbits, and gray squirrel—birds and animals I could bag with the little .410 shotgun. One fall the big gray bandtailed wild pigeons arrived in the Agua Fria country in force. They numbered in the thousands, and huge flocks of them would fly up and down the canyon landing in the groves of oak trees where they feasted on ripe acorns. At times so many would land in a single tree its branches would droop with their weight.

With prospects of a change of diet I knocked off work early one afternoon, and armed with the little shotgun, started out to obtain the ingredients for a wild pigeon stew. It was not as simple as it sounds, the pigeons were wary, and the killing range of a .410 shotgun is mighty short. I climbed and sneaked, and each time I would get almost in shooting distance the birds would take off with a roar of wings.

But now and then a bird which was either unlucky or stupid would fly close enough to provide me a shot, and by sundown I had four fat pigeons. They had stuffed themselves with ripe acorns so large it seemed impossible a bird their size could swallow them. Carefully I plucked and cleaned the pigeons, and Dot soaked them overnight in cold salt water to help take away any wild taste.

Next evening Dot placed the pigeons in a roasting pan and baked them with all the trimmings. Their meat was dark and fat, their aroma while cooking, rich and appetizing. Then we sat down to eat them, but a single bite was enough. The meat was so bitter we couldn't swallow it—they tasted exactly like the acorns upon which they had been feeding. Even the dog wouldn't eat the damned things, and supper that night ended up being bacon and eggs.

But there were many items the woods and streams gave us that were real delicacies. It's hard to beat a pan of crisp fried, fresh-caught rainbow trout—and they were there for the catching.

In addition to fried trout, smoked trout are something hard

to beat. Red Whiskers rigged up a smokehouse and smoked trout by the dozen. We ate our share of them, along with an occasional haunch of venison. He said he had learned the trick of smoking meat as a boy in Finland, and although I never learned his secret, I have never eaten better smoked fish or meat.

In fall the buckeye tree bears a nut much like a large, golfball-sized chestnut. I never tried to eat them, in fact I always had the idea they were at least mildly poisonous, yet one fellow who camped there on the Agua Fria, living from hand to mouth, did roast and eat them.

Another sniper, whom we knew briefly, dug tule roots and roasted them after carefully washing and peeling them. I tried them once, but to me they tasted like thick mud-flavored wall-paper paste.

There were pine nuts, and hazel nuts in the higher country, but seldom did the miners along the rivers take time to gather them. So many of them were city bred, driven to mining for a living by necessity, and they really did not know nor appreciate the out-of-doors.

They worked on the river, really saw little of the beauty or the things of interest around them, and lived on a diet of hot-cakes, bacon, and beans.

CHAPTER IX

IT'S TOUGH TO BREAK CAMP

THE WINTER FLOODS WERE PAST, AND WITH SPRING RAINS NOW drawing to a close, the Agua Fria was rapidly receding to its normal summer flow.

Low gravel bars and bedrock along the stream bottom were once again becoming exposed and workable, but during the two years we had been on the river many changes had taken place.

Spots which once had produced good days' wages for us were worked out—the gold was gone. There were many more people along the river now than when we had first arrived. Likely places we had intended to work suddenly sprouted camps and were taken over by other snipers. Certainly they had as much right to those places as Dot and I did, but as a result, we often were reduced to working spots we had previously passed over because they produced such poor pay. In fact, during April and early May when we should have been making two or three dollars a day, we found ourselves lucky to average as much as a dollar for a day's hard work.

Our decision came one evening after supper as I sat at the tenthouse table carefully weighing out our day's earnings on the gold scales. The tiny mound of fine yellow flakes which spilled onto the scales, representing more than eight hours toil, came to just four cents less than a dollar.

Disgustedly, I slammed my hand on the table, making the

gold scales jump. "To hell with it—let's get outa this damned starvation country before it gets any worse!"

Almost before the words were out of my mouth I regretted them, for I expected my wife to flare up. I knew Dot had come to love this country, and to her, our little tenthouse, small and crude though it was, had truly become home.

Dot turned, her hands wet with dishwater, and looked at me.

"You know, I've been going to suggest something like that for the last couple weeks," she said, "but I was afraid you wouldn't agree. Only question is, where shall we go?"

That she was not only agreeable to the idea of moving, but had been thinking for the past couple weeks of suggesting it, left me somewhat taken aback. Suddenly, it was I who was at loss for an answer.

"Well, almost any place would beat this . . . There's the Stanislaus and the Mokelumne Rivers over in Tuolumne and Calaveras County, and there's the American on up farther . . . But, when I was a kid the Yuba River up around Downieville in Sierra County was pretty good. How would you like to give that area a whirl?" It was a pretty superfluous question, for Dot wasn't even too sure where in what county Downieville might be located, and certainly she had no idea of what mining possibilities it might offer. The decision, whether I liked it or not, was mine, and all I could do was hope it was the right one.

But to talk of moving and to actually make the move itself are two different things—even when home is nothing more than a tenthouse. We sat up late that night making plans. There was no use postponing things, we agreed, and next morning would be none too soon to get started. Yet, when morning came it required more than a little intestinal fortitude to take that first step toward leaving.

The first thing we discovered was that we did not even begin to have enough packing boxes. Neither of us had realized how much we had accumulated over the past two years in the way of clothing, equipment, tools, and just the odds and ends that go with housekeeping. We had arrived with little more than tent, stove, suitcases, and a bed, but now not only was the tenthouse fairly bulging, it had overflowed to a small storage shed I had built several months before.

Dot began packing clothing and dishes while I started loading sluice boxes, tools, and other mining equipment on the trailer. There was pump and hose to load, picks, shovels, crowbars, and other tools. But before we were halfway through our loading I had to unhook the trailer and make a special trip to town for more boxes in which to pack the remainder of our belongings.

I returned from town to find Bill McCarty at camp, highly indignant because we had not told anyone we were leaving.

"What the hell you trying to do, Jess—run out on us? Taking off like this isn't even fair. We should have at least been able to get together and throw a goin' away party or something."

But despite his grumbling, Bill pitched in and began helping me carry the heavier items to the trailer. By now the camp had begun to take on a bare look, and the most disturbed of anyone was poor little Ladybug. The dog knew something was brewing. There was change and break of routine she did not like and could not fathom. She trotted from one spot to another, into the tenthouse and out again, nervous and agitated. Finally for lack of a better place she jumped into the front seat of the Chevvy where she sat nervously watching every move Dot and I made.

Noon, the tenthouse, reduced to simply a rough lumber skeleton, stood stark and almost indecent in the spring sunlight. The last boxes had been stowed aboard, the tent itself lashed down as a tarpaulin over the trailer to protect its load. We stood there, just the three of us, Bill, who had become our closest friend, Dot and I, and munched cold sandwiches Dot had throw together before she packed the last of the food and cooking utensils.

It was hard to find something to say. We were leaving this

place and our friends where we had been happy for two years. The garden plot where Dot had raised vegetables and waged war with deer and raccoons stood ready for tilling, and water tinkled softly from overhanging rocks into the little pool that formed our spring. The trail to the river seemed to stand out more distinctly against the green grass, and the soft, hushed noise of the river, flowing along its rocky channel, also seemed suddenly more noticeable.

The campsite itself was neat and clean, for we had left not a paper or tin can, or speck of trash of any kind. Dot, silly as it might have seemed, had even carefully swept the tenthouse floor after Bill and I removed the tent from it.

"Well hell, Bill," I said, "I guess there's no use standing here. We gotta long way to go and I guess we might as well get going." We shook hands, and Dot suddenly embarrassed poor old Bill by kissing him goodbye.

The old Chevvy's engine roared to life, and with Ladybug barking and Dot and me waving, we started up the hill. I looked back once and Bill was still standing there waving, a tall, dark man whom I wondered if we would ever see again.

As the Chevvy labored up the steep grade, the well-laden trailer slowing its progress a bit more than usual, I wondered who would be moving into our camp now that we were gone. And I wondered how long it would be before Cap, the old buzzard, would come prowling furtively down the river to pick up anything we might have left behind. It's tough to break camp, particularly when it's a camp you have enjoyed. About the only satisfaction I could derive from it was that when old Cap did arrive, he would find damned slim pickings.

We stopped in Mariposa, cashed in the last of our gold, and withdrew our small savings account from the bank. At least we could say this: when we came to Mariposa and the Agua Fria it was with little more than the clothes on our backs. We were leaving with a bank account, money in our pockets, and the knowledge we could be self-sufficient in any country where we could mine gold.

Our plan was to drive to Ceres, stop and see my dad and tell him of our plans to move, then start for Sierra County the following day.

It was nearly dark by the time we reached Ceres, and both Dot and I were bone tired. Nevertheless, Dad kept us up what seemed like half the night, talking over our latest experiences and of our coming plans. Finally, around midnight we crawled into bed, grateful for the happy reunion and a place to stay, but so tired we both could have slept a week. But habit is hard to overcome, and next morning at 6 A.M., just as if someone had set off an alarm, I was wide awake and ready to get going. I tried to lie still so Dot could sleep for a while, but suddenly I realized she was just as wide awake as I was.

By 7:30 we had finished breakfast, but Dad urged us to stay with him another day. True, we had shopping to do, and the Chevvy needed a new set of sparkplugs and points. The deciding factor, however, was that if we spent the day in Ceres we could leave before daylight the following morning and get through the valley before the heat of midday.

Dad took Dot shopping while I worked over the Chevvy, even to the point of giving it a thorough grease job and washing it. The day vanished rapidly, and at 9 P.M. that night we crawled into bed with the alarm clock set for 2 A.M.

The next thing I remember was the alarm clock rattling, and Dad stirring around in the kitchen making coffee. We rolled out of bed, sipped cups of scalding black coffee, and a half hour later in the early morning darkness we said our goodbyes and pulled out of the yard, headed for Sierra County.

On up Highway 99, through Modesto and Ripon, through a sleepy, early-morning Stockton we rolled, and the first lights began appearing in kitchen windows of farmhouses as we reached the outskirts of Lodi. The air was cool and exhilarating, and as we drove along in the half light of summer dawn the rich aroma of new hay, of willows, of freshly turned soil, and the myriad other valley smells began building up a sense of suppressed excitement in us.

We stopped at a gas station and restaurant on the outskirts of Sacramento just as the first rays of the sun were breaking over the crest of the Sierra to the east. I filled the gas tank, and throwing economy to the winds, we went into the restuarant and ordered breakfast of ham and eggs with all the trimmings.

From Sacramento eastward the foothills begin to rise, almost imperceptibly at first, then they soon grow into rolling hills sprinkled with stands of white oak and occasional Digger pine.

But, soon, as we traveled along old Highway 40 and passed Roseville, the hills became distinct, and we could see the real mountains lying to the north and east. By the time we reached Auburn we were back in the Mother Lode gold country again, and there we left Highway 40 and branched off on narrow, winding Highway 49, headed for Grass Valley, Nevada City, and eventually Downieville.

And as we neared Grass Valley the country changed again, with tall green Ponderosa pine and big-leafed black oaks replacing the blue-gray Digger pines and the white oaks of the valley country. There also was a change in the air, for while summer had been only a step away in the foothill country of Mariposa County, we were now in the edge of the mountains where wild flowers were blooming, and it was still spring.

We stopped in Grass Valley for gasoline, for this was the last place we could buy it at valley prices, then headed on into the mountains, and crossed the divide into the Yuba River drainage.

And mountains they truly are. The highway, narrow and winding, clung precariously to slopes so steep it was questionable whether a newcomer to the area would describe them as cliffs or hillsides. This was not the California of easy living which the Spaniard found and developed long before the first American ever crossed the Sierra. Nor were these the benevolent foothills we had known in the Agua Fria country. This, I knew full well, was country that would fight back; this was country that could kill you.

We dropped down the steep grade to the North Fork of the Yuba River, and followed the winding highway up the river canyon.

Anyone who remembers the event will have to admit we arrived in the town of Downieville with a bang. There appeared to be only one parking place on the tree-bordered main street large enough to park both the Chevvy and trailer, and, as I pulled into the open space I found out why it had remained vacant. I eased the Chevvy into the curb beside a large locust tree, looking back as much as I did forward to make sure the trailer was coming in as it should. Suddenly, the Chevvy came to an abrupt halt with a clattering, tinny crash, and although I could not see what I had hit, I knew full well that a fender had suffered damage. I jumped out, and inspection revealed that the innocent appearing locust tree standing at the curb contained a built-in booby trap for newcomers. Just above the curb, at fender height, a large nob stuck out from the bole of the tree, and I could tell by its scars and spots of missing bark that my old Chevvy was not the first to come into contact with it.

At sound of the crash people came pouring out of stores and the town saloon. "Well—another new one's hit town," someone shouted, but they were all laughing and friendly, and while Ladybug barked at all the commotion and Dot worried about whether the Chevvy would still run, a couple of men helped me pry the fender away from the wheel. Damage, once the fender was pried and bent back into a semblance of its normal shape, was negligible.

Downieville lies on the banks of the North Fork of the Yuba River at its confluence with Downie Creek, and it is the county seat of Sierra County. I doubt that in 1936 it had a population of two hundred people.

The town, simply a gold mining camp about 1850, was first known as Durgan's Flat, and another camp located across the river from it was known as Jersey Flat. However, as a Major Downie, one of the early arrivals, became a leading citizen, the camp which soon had a population of about five thousand, became known as Downieville.

And Downieville has the dubious distinction of being the only gold camp in the length and breadth of California's Mother Lode in which, during those hectic gold rush days, a woman was tried and hanged.

The hanging occurred on July 5, 1851, when a luckless young Mexican woman, by the name of Juanita, sometimes described as a dance hall girl, sometimes as something worse, stabbed a miner in her small shack located on the edge of the town's red-light district.

Whether the stabbing was justified has never been resolved. It was enough that the woman was Mexican, that her paramour was a gambler, and Fred Cannon, victim of the knifing, although admittedly drunk at the time, was a well-known and well-liked American miner. Within hours the woman was formally charged, dragged before a kangaroo court of miners, and by noon was found guilty and sentenced to death. The hanging occurred on the Jersey Flat Bridge. A noose simply was slipped around the woman's neck and its other end tied to a bridge girder. Then, before a mob of a thousand drunken, excitement-hungry miners, gamblers, whores, and hangers-on, the hangman simply shoved Juanita off the bridge.

But not all of the stories of crime and justice in Downieville ended in tragedy or bloodshed.

Articles of apparel and clothing were hard to come by in those early mining days, and when it happened one day that a miner was caught stealing a pair of boots, he was duly arrested and hauled before the justice of the peace. The justice, who also happened to be the proprietor of a saloon, selected a jury from among his bar patrons and declared that trial was underway in his barroom.

Normally, the man found guilty of theft of an article such as a pair of boots could look forward to at least a horeswhipping and to being run out of town.

The court action was short and very much to the point. The complaining witness testified, the boots were shown as evidence, and the jury was less than moments in finding the defendant guilty. However, there was some indecision among the jurors as to exactly what penalty should be invoked. While they discussed this matter further, they ordered the now guilty defendant to buy a round of drinks. The drinks were ordered and everyone, including judge, jurors, and onlookers, imbibed. The defendant ordered a second round, and then a third for the house. In fact, before the afternoon ended occupants of the saloon, including judge and jury, were well under the influence. They sobered up later in the evening to find the defendant had left town. He also had left without paying for the drinks, and he had taken the disputed boots with him!

The Chevvy fender was repaired, or at least restored to where I could drive the car again. Then with considerable good-natured kidding, the fellows who helped me beat and pry the fender back into shape, escorted Dot and me across the street to the town restaurant.

As we ate, we learned that a man had some cabins about a mile upriver from town which he rented to snipers for ten dollars a month. And, although ten dollars was maybe a little more than we felt we would have liked to pay, we decided to rent one anyway and eliminate cramped tenthouse living.

Our rented cabin was hidden in a grove of tall Ponderosa pines and Douglas fir on a little flat about a hundred yards from the North Fork of the Yuba. It contained two rooms, a combination kitchen-living room and a small bedroom, and in July or August it probably would have been a delightful place for a summer vacation. The cabin porch overlooked the clear, tumbling mountain stream.

But the location was on a north slope which in winter and spring was seldom touched by sun, and even in early June it was still cold and dismal. The cabin and everything around it was damp and clammy, for it had not been lived in for at least two or three months. When we opened the doors and windows to let the building air out, and built a fire in the wood stove, the interior of the cabin was so damp that big beads of moisture built up on the walls.

Even getting firewood was a problem, for there on the north slope every piece of dead wood that normally would have burned well was damp and punky from the spring rains. While Dot finished unpacking I drove back across the bridge and found a sunny hillside where dry wood was abundant, and during the afternoon I cut a fair-sized load and hauled it home.

Probably the one chore in all of our years of mining that I detested the most was that of woodcutting. It was a job that had to be done, and I usually set aside one afternoon each week for it. While I cut wood Dot usually washed clothes, a job which was just as necessary but just as thankless as my woodcutting chore. Those afternoons of washing and woodcutting came to be known as the afternoons that we spent "rustling feed for a dead horse."

With camp finally settled and the cabin at least partially dried out, we arose the following morning intent on getting our gold-mining operation underway. While in town the previous day several people had told us about a huge earthslide—a virtual avalanche—which had come down Hungry Mouth Gulch during the winter.

So great had been the slide that for several hours it blocked flow of the North Fork of the Yuba itself, forming a huge reservoir. The boulders and trash which formed the dam finally gave way, and water went bursting downstream, washing and gullying the river channel, and almost flooding Downieville.

In the wake of the slide and flood, snipers flocked to the river to determine if new areas of bedrock had washed clear and to see what the avalanche itself might have exposed.

Hungry Mouth Gulch had gotten its name in gold rush days from the fact that it contained virtually no evidence of gold, but when the slide occurred, much to the surprise of everyone, it apparently carried with it a huge pocket of quartz gold, and spewed it for a mile along the stream and hillside. For several weeks the miners had picked up pieces of gold, some weighing several ounces, and even now, they told us, snipers were finding pieces of the big pocket which had been spilled by the slide.

With this information in mind, Dot, Ladybug, and I started up the river next morning, armed with pick, shovel, and gold pan, to try and find a place that might carry pay dirt. All morning long we prospected and dug, coming up with a few fine colors, but nothing of any true worth or of any real promise. Around noon, we neared the junction of the river and Hungry Mouth Gulch. Huge boulders, some as big as houses, had spewed down in the avalanche and lodged in the river.

Great pine trees, broken and battered, along with brush and debris, had swept down the mountainside in the avalanche, and in places the bottom of the main river canyon resembled a giant pile of jackstraws. Miners had moved into the area in the wake of the slide, and there were a dozen camps near the confluence of Hungry Mouth Gulch and the river.

We prospected here and there, and upon rounding a bend in the stream bed we happened onto a camp where a young man and woman were preparing lunch. The couple called out a greeting to us and insisted we have coffee with them. They had been mining along the North Fork for nearly a year, and had been there when the slide came roaring down Hungry Mouth Gulch. But although they were among the first to hear of the gold discovery, their luck had not been exactly remarkable. They had found several pieces of quartz gold scattered by the slide, but none apparently was very large, and certainly not overly numerous. From what we could ascertain, there had been quite a quantity of gold found as result of the avalanche, but very few individuals had found any large amount.

In fact, I doubt that most of the people who mined Hungry Mouth Gulch after the slide made any more money over the long haul than those who simply sniped the river, picking up whatever fine gold happened to catch in their sluice boxes.

All morning long, as we had traveled upcanyon on our prospecting expedition I had idly noticed that a pretty fair-sized cloudbank was building up. Now, as we finished our coffee and prepared to leave our hosts' camp, I realized the clouds were even heavier, and that a light breeze had sprung up. Nevertheless, we continued on, finally turning into Hungry Mouth Gulch itself.

We had traveled about a half mile up the gulch from the North Fork of the Yuba when we reached the upper edge of the slide area. There we stopped to prospect a little side gully which was strewn with rubble and broken quartz rock. I took several pans without raising a single color of gold, and had actually given up when Dot, working a few yards up the hill from me, let out an excited yell. In her hand she held a piece of quartz about as big around and as long as a man's little finger. It was exactly half white quartz rock and half gold.

Excitement of the discovery spurred us on, and not until it began to rain did we even consider quitting. However, our efforts netted us not another single fleck or speck of gold, and by the time we headed back toward camp our clothes already were wet, and it was beginning to rain harder.

Before we reached camp the rain had turned to snow, and the last mile of travel along the stream bed was slow and treacherous. A slip on that slick, wet rock could mean a badly sprained ankle, broken leg, or worse.

We arrived back in camp cold, soaked to the skin, exhausted, and not even too enthused about Dot's discovery of the twenty-dollar quartz nugget, for we knew it was simply a fluke. We might work there another month and never find another flake of gold. Then, with dusk falling and snow coming down even harder, we found that the roof of our rented cabin leaked in a half-dozen places, including a spot right over our bed, and our blankets, during the afternoon, had become soaked.

We spent the night stoking the fire and trying to dry out blankets, with cans and buckets set at strategic spots to catch the various drips. The only good thing that happened was that before morning, it stopped raining.

For the next several days we prospected, patched the cabin roof, and cut wood in order to keep a fire burning almost constantly in the cabin stove. As soon as the cabin cooled off the dampness crept back into it, and it took on the odor of moisture and mildew. It was not a very pleasant place in which to live, and certainly did not even begin to be as warm or cozy as our little tenthouse.

We worked two or three spots, and prospected a half dozen more, but the best we produced during the next several days was an average of about fifty cents for eight hours hard work —hardly enough to pay for bacon and beans. Unlike the Agua Fria country where it generally was all right for a sniper to work anywhere along the river, a good many portions of the North Fork of the Yuba were taken up by valid mining claims which were heavily posted against trespassing, and zealously protected by their owners.

Yet, I was not really discouraged about the mining prospects here, for I knew there was good mining ground in the Downieville area. It was simply a matter of finding it, and of getting permission to mine it if it happened to be under private ownership. However, even though I had confidence that this country would produce gold for us, I also felt something of a sense of urgency. At the moment we were not supporting ourselves from our mining, but were living off our small savings.

Saturday arrived. We had been in Sierra County for just a bit longer than a week, and we decided it was time to go to town. There were a couple of men there whom I had known years ago, when I visited Downieville with my family, as a boy. Furthermore, we had to find another place to rent. The cabin in which we were living was just too cold and damp.

CHAPTER X

SIERRA COUNTY

DURING THOSE DEPRESSION DAYS IN SIERRA COUNTY'S DOWNIEville area Tony Lavazolla was the miners' friend. Big, balding, barrel-chested Tony was owner and operator of Downieville's single hostelry, the St. Charles Hotel. But Tony also was town constable and operator of the town's leading saloon.

Tony was unofficial mayor of Downieville, town greeter, served as parade marshal on the Fourth of July, and in any other necessary capacity when the occasion arose. Tony and Judge Robbins, who was town barber and justice of the peace, were among the selected few always consulted by other county officials before they made any move or decision affecting the Downieville area. Tony loved mining and was a collector of rare specimens of gold, but first of all, Tony was a humanitarian.

No down-and-out sniper ever went hungry if Tony Lavazolla knew of his plight. Tony had a special place in his heart for mining men, and particularly for the snipers who scratched out a living with gold pan and sluice box along the Yuba River. He helped them out whenever he could.

I had known Tony and Judge Robbins since the days when, as a boy, I spent summer vacations along the Yuba River near Downieville with my parents. Naturally, they were the ones I sought out when I found myself in need of information regarding a place to stay and a spot in which to mine.

Tony was deeply involved in some kind of mining conversation with a lone bar patron and did not immediately look up when Dot and I entered his saloon, which was a part of the old hotel. I had not seen Tony for more than four years, but he had changed little.

Tony finally glanced in our direction, did a sudden double-take, and the next instant my hand was being crushed in one of his big bear paws, and his other big hand was pounding me on the back.

"Jess Coffey—old Java. How the hell are you, and what in hell are you doing up in this country?"

I managed to get a word in edgewise, introduced Dot, whom Tony had never met, and told him about having turned sniper and what we were doing there.

"Well—by God, it's good to have you here—and we'll find you a place to live. As for a place to mine—hell, I've got a couple claims up the river a ways that should carry a color or two, that you're more than welcome to mine. Let's go see Judge Robbins and find out what he knows about a cabin for you to stay in," said Tony.

Leaving his saloon completely unattended with the single customer still sitting at the bar, Tony escorted us across the street to Judge Robbins's barber shop, which suddenly became the scene of a second reunion. Yes, the judge knew of a place we could rent, in fact he had a cabin of his own downstream from Goodyear Bar which he would let us have, just so somebody would be living in it and taking care of it. We almost had to insist that he accept five dollars per month rent. In addition, said the judge, there was a stretch of river bar a short distance down from the cabin which he felt should provide pretty fair wages if we used pump and sluice box.

With directions drawn on the back of an envelope by Judge Robbins, Dot and I climbed into the Chevvy and headed for the cabin we hoped to live in. We arrived to find that it sat on a small pine- and oak-clad flat overlooking the river. It was clean, warm, and dry, and to us, it could have been the St. Francis Hotel in San Francisco.

The cabin consisted of a 12 x 16 combination kitchen-living room, a bedroom nearly as large, and a third room somewhat smaller that we used as a storage area. The cabin already was furnished with stove, bed, tables, and chairs. In addition, there was a nearby shed to provide storage for my mining equipment, firewood, and shelter for the old Chevvy. The thing Dot liked about the cabin in addition to its spaciousness, was the fact it had lots of windows overlooking the river, and a wide railed porch.

While Dot swept out our new dwelling, which already was quite clean, I made a quick survey of the river bar and concluded after a few sample pans of gravel, that it probably would pay pretty good dividends in fine gold. During the early mining days numerous hydraulic mines had operated in the Downieville area. The old-timers had used nozzles which directed water under terrific pressure against banks of gold-bearing gravel. Millions of tons of gravel were washed out, and while the original miners recovered a large share of the gold, much of the fine gold gushed on through their sluice boxes with the mine tailings, and was deposited in the river. It was these old mine tailings and this fine gold that we would be dumping into our own sluice box, in the hope of recovering what the old-timers had lost.

We headed back to town, excited as a pair of schoolkids over our turn of good luck, and quickly told Judge Robbins of our satisfaction with the cabin. I also informed Tony that it appeared we had a place to mine which would be closer to the cabin than his claim, and we would take a raincheck on his mining property.

Tony, who had immediately taken a liking to Dot, poured her and himself a glass of wine, then motioned for me to follow him into the small storeroom in the rear of the bar.

Among cases of beer, stacks of empty bottles, and other paraphernalia of the storeroom was a row of several large sacks which appeared to be filled with food packages and groceries. Tony picked up one of the larger sacks which must have weighed nearly forty pounds, and handed it to me.

"Now, dammit, Jess—you take this, and I don't want any argument from you," Tony informed me. "I keep these here just to help out a miner now and then when he's hit a little run of bad luck, or when he's just getting started. You can use this now, and it's not that I care so damn much about you —you could get along eating acorns and jackrabbits—but that's a pretty damn fine girl you got there and I want to see that she makes out all right."

No amount of argument would change Tony's mind, and rather than hurt his feelings, we took the big bag of groceries. Actually, they came in darned handy, for since coming to Sierra County we had been forced to dip into our savings to help buy groceries. The sack contained such staples as bacon, beans, potatoes, flour, syrup, and other necessities.

We spent the remainder of the afternoon and early evening moving camp from the damp, drafty cabin to Judge Robbins's cabin on the river bluff. Actually, it was not too difficult this time, because most of our stuff had not yet been unpacked, and this time there was no tenthouse to tear down. By the time darkness arrived we were pretty comfortably set up in our new home. Actually, in a cabin as large as our new abode we were almost lost. Two whole, large rooms and a big storage area all to ourselves was wonderful.

The weather suddenly had warmed up that day, and we were bone-tired from our hectic siege of moving. After supper, we moved a couple chairs out onto the wide, railed porch which overlooked the river and the broad, steep, timbered hillside to the southwest. A lopsided new moon was breaking over the ridgetop, silhouetting the rugged mountain crest, and below us we could hear the river churning softly along the rough, boulder-strewn stream bed. "You know, I think I'm going to like this place even better than the Agua Fria, and, we're going to find some pretty good gold here too, I'll just bet you," commented Dot. "Sure we are," I told her. "Those were some pretty good sample pans I got here today. We're going to hit some good-paying ground tomorrow." And, as I said it, I only wished that I was as positive as I sounded.

Long before the sun was touching the river next morning, I was busy setting up my sluice box and getting my pump and gasoline engine ready for operation. By the time Dot arrived after taking care of her housekeeping chores I had our first day's mining well underway. All morning long I kept a steady flow of gravel running through the box. Noon came, but instead of pausing for lunch, I shut down motor and pump and proceeded to clean up the sluice box to determine how profitable our morning had been.

Carefully, I lifted the screen riffles and washed down the sluice box, its contents filtering into a gold pan which Dot held at its lower end. Even as the fine black sand which had caught in the riffles was washing down the box I could see traces of gold. Finally, the box was clean, and taking the gold pan from Dot, I swirled it carefully in the clear, cold water. Each time I swirled the pan the streak of yellow metal which trailed behind the black sand in the pan, grew wider, and in addition to the fine gold, two match-head-sized nuggets appeared.

I estimated our morning's work had netted us more than a full pennyweight—nearly two dollars' worth of gold. Judge Robbins's calculations had been correct—this section of the river did contain gold in good, workable amounts, and not all of it was in fine flake form, either.

For more than a month we worked that one small section of stream, averaging about three dollars per day, and when it had finally been exhausted, we moved downstream a quarter of a mile to another section that proved equally good.

The second morning we were in Judge Robbins's cabin I awakened just after daylight with Dot nudging me in the ribs.

"Wake up—we've inherited livestock with our new home, and it's demanding to be fed."

I raised up on one elbow and looked out the window to find myself staring at a big, bushy-tailed gray squirrel who was sitting on the window sill, rattling his claws on the glass pane. His chattering left no question about what he wanted. He wanted something to eat—and he wanted it now.

Dot climbed out of bed, went into the kitchen and found a couple of walnuts. Sliding the window open slightly, she placed the nuts on the sill, then stepped back to watch the proceedings. When she opened the window the squirrel leaped down, ran across the porch and perched on the rail, but a moment later he was back on the window sill, investigating his breakfast. Apparently the nuts were exactly what he wanted, for with the ease of an expert he cracked them, fished out the meat and ate it. Our visitor then climbed back on the porch railing and proceeded to scold Ladybug, who had come to investigate what all the noise was about.

The squirrel became a part of our family, arriving each morning to noisily demand breakfast.

We learned from Judge Robbins that the squirrel had been the pet of the people who had rented the cabin before us.

So regularly did he awaken us just at daylight that we came to regard him as our alarm clock. The big squirrel regarded Ladybug with the same disdain that snobbish aristocracy holds for the lowest of peasants, and after he became a bit more acquainted with our household he would not even waste breath berating her.

While I operated sluice box and pump on the gravel bar below the cabin Dot often went exploring for places which she could mine. She had her own small sluice box which she used at times when she found a bit of good, workable ground.

We had been in Sierra County about a month when on one particular morning, Dot, accompanied by Ladybug, began prospecting downstream about a hundred yards below where I was working. There she discovered a small section of shallow bedrock in which there were a number of crevices that panned quite well. The bedrock had been uncovered by the past winter's floods which left a high wall of gravel standing at the edge of it. The gravel wall was at least ten feet high, composed of round, washed rock which ranged in size from pebbles to pieces as large as cantaloupes. The steep river hillside studded with loose rock extended upward beyond the gravel, and there, unknown to Dot, dwelled a family of ground squirrels.

Ladybug was not particular what she chased. Lizard, chipmunks, rabbits, anything that would run suited her just right, and ground squirrels were among her favorite quarry. Dot, busy on hands and knees cleaning the bedrock crevices, did not notice the ground squirrel that went scurrying across the hillside above the gravel bank, but Ladybug, always alert for such happenings, did see it. Without even bothering to yip, she shot up the gravel bank and gave chase. The squirrel, a real professional at evading such assaults, saw her coming and darted down into his burrow.

Ladybug, only a jump behind the fleeing squirrel as he disappeared down the hole, began digging at the mouth of the burrow with both front paws like a miniature bulldozer.

Dirt and rocks cascaded down, hit other loose rocks, started them rolling, and the whole mess now a miniature avalanche, slammed into the ten-foot gravel wall and started it caving. Dot had her back to the wall of gravel and the first thing she knew of impending danger was when falling rocks hit her on the bottom and back, and others began tumbling down and building up around her feet and legs.

Dot jumped up, tried to run, but the gravel embankment, now falling in even greater volume, trapped her until she was nearly waist deep in rocks and rubble. Try as she might she could not extricate herself.

It was not my wife's shouts, but the sound of rolling rock and the cloud of dust and sand it kicked up that attracted my attention. I was not sure what was happening, but I took off on a dead run for the scene of the avalanche. When I arrived Dot still had not fully extricated herself, and Ladybug, ignoring the havoc she had created, was still busily engaged in trying to dig out the ground squirrel and still was sending a pretty good shower of rocks tumbling down.

I hollered at the dog and finally, through threats and curses, managed to get her to desist her ground-squirrel excavating. By scraping rocks from around her legs I managed to free my wife, who by now was both angry and scared.

Then, to show her she really had meant no harm, Ladybug came dashing down the hill, knocking down more loose rocks, to wag her stubby tail, lick Dot's face, and congratulate her on her narrow escape.

An hour later with her composure somewhat recovered, Dot moved off downstream searching for another likely place to mine. The spot she found was beneath a huge boulder, about a hundred yards from where Ladybug had caused the rockslide. Winter flood waters had undermined the huge rock which was nearly four feet thick, and almost twice that wide. Shaped something like a giant loaf of bread, one end of the big rock extended seven or eight feet out from the gravel riverbank, the water having washed beneath it, exposing a patch of soft and somewhat decomposed bedrock.

The big boulder was about four feet above the level of the bedrock and it was easy for Dot to crawl beneath it and fill her gold pan with fine, broken bits of the bedrock which she hoped had collected gold. And Dot's hopes were fulfilled. Her very first pan netted her nearly fifty cents, and a second one was just as good. With such lucrative results at hand, Dot walked back upstream to get me, for a dozen pans of rich bedrock such as she had found would amount to more than I could make all day with pump and sluice box.

We worked diligently for an hour beneath the boulder, digging farther and farther back beneath it, each pan of the soft bedrock we washed produced from twenty-five to fifty cents or more. It appeared we were going to have a highly profitable day. Then, because it was shady for her beneath the rock and because I used a larger gold pan and panned faster than she did anyway, I suggested to Dot that she stay beneath the rock and scrape the bedrock and fine gravel into a pile and that I pan it.

Dot had been under the big boulder only a short while when I noticed out of the corner of my eye that Ladybug, who, since the rockslide episode, had been lying quietly in the shade of a nearby bush, had gotten up and was sniffing inquisitively at the rocky, gravel wall which held the boulder in place.

Suddenly, the little fox terrier began to bark furiously, running first to my wife, then to the wall of rock in which the big boulder was embedded. Dot dropped the light prospecting pick she was using and paused to watch the excited little dog, but when she did not actually move, the dog grabbed her pants leg and began tugging on it.

"Let go of me, you crazy little mutt," said Dot, half-irritated at Ladybug's sudden antics. "What do you think you're trying to do—let go of me!" But instead of letting go of Dot's pants leg, the dog braced her feet and pulled even harder, growling and whining as she yanked frantically at the pants.

So sudden had been the assault that Dot had been caught somewhat off balance. Trying to shove Ladybug away from her and at the same time not fall down, she had traveled sort of crab-fashion on hands and knees some four or five feet from beneath the overhanging rock. Suddenly, as Dot moved clear of the rock, the little dog let go of her pants leg and leaped into her lap, barking, whining excitedly, and trying to lick her face.

At that instant it happened. Without warning, without a sound except the earth-shaking "thud" when it hit the bedrock, the huge boulder which weighed at least a dozen tons, fell on the very spot where Dot had been kneeling only a moment before.

Dot and I stood there transfixed, for without a doubt she had missed death by a matter of seconds. And there was no doubt that somehow the little dog had sensed the impending danger and saved Dot's life. Beneath the rock were Dot's pick, shovel, and gold pan, flattened, smashed to splinters, where I suppose they still lie today.

Reaction set in, Dot trembled as if taken by a sudden chill, and silently she began to cry. She picked up Ladybug and clasped her to her chest, with salty tears streaming down her cheeks which Ladybug tried to lick away.

"What do you do with a dog like this," asked Dot, a wry smile creeping through her tears, "a dog that one minute nearly buries you in an avalanche, and the next minute saves your life?"

I felt almost as shocked and shaken as Dot did, for it had been a truly narrow escape.

"Come on, honey," I told her. "Let's get out of here and go home—let's not push our luck any further—we've had all the excitement we need for one day."

But it was not yet noon when we arrived back at the cabin, and the day still held more than a little excitement for us. I prepared lunch while Dot bathed and applied iodine to numerous scratches and abrasions received in the avalanche, and after eating, I persuaded her to lie down for a while.

With Dot resting, it seemed an opportune time had arrived for me to do some wood gathering. With Ladybug at my heels, I started off with the ax to find some suitable oak or manzanita for the fire. The trouble with Ladybug was that she seldom spent much time trotting at my heels. A lizard scuttling off through the dry leaves, a squirrel or rabbit, or even just the fancied scent or sound of bird or animal was enough to send her dashing off in pursuit.

Before I had traveled more than a couple hundred yards the little dog had already been off on at least a couple short excursions. And, as I located a large dead oak tree and began trimming limbs off it, she took off a third time through the scattered brush beyond me. Busily swinging the ax, I paid scant attention to the dog, who was rummaging around in the leaves some twenty-five yards from where I was working.

Suddenly, the cry that Ladybug made was more of a startled squeal of surprise and pain than it was a bark or howl. Her first frightened yelp was followed by a series of high-pitched cries and yips, and although I could not see the dog, I dropped the ax and ran toward her, for I knew she was hurt and in trouble. Instantly I thought of a rattlesnake, I was sure she had been struck by one. But, as I rounded a low bush I came upon her thrashing and struggling in the leaves and trampled bracken. Her left front leg was locked in the jaws of a large coyote trap.

Kneeling beside the struggling dog I grabbed her and pulled her to me, and was promptly bitten for my troubles, for she was now beside herself with pain and fear. But when I shouted and slapped her lightly, it seemed to bring Ladybug to her senses and she quit fighting me. I grabbed the trap, one of its heavy springs in each hand, and placed it across my knee. With all my strength I compressed the springs until its steel jaws opened, releasing the dog's foot.

Under normal circumstances a trap so large would have shattered the bone in the little terrier's slender leg, but a quirk of fate had worked in her favor. A small oak twig about the size of a pencil had also been caught in the trap jaws and had prevented them from closing completely. Forgetting both ax and wood I picked up the injured animal and carried her to the cabin. Dot, awakened by our sudden arrival, spent the remainder of the afternoon bathing Ladybug's injured paw in warm Epsom salts water.

Later in the afternoon I went back to retrieve my ax, and paused to more fully examine the coyote trap in which Ladybug had been caught. It was an unusually large one, and had probably been set the previous winter by some trapper who had forgotten it. I again placed the trap across my knee and gripped the springs in each hand as I had done to release the dog earlier in the day. But, try as I might, even though I exerted every ounce of strength I had, I could not force those jaws apart even an inch. How, in that moment of stress when the dog was caught, I managed to find the strength to open the trap, I do not know.

I unfastened the trap from the tree to which it had been wired and carried it home with me, hanging it on the cabin wall outside the door. It hung there all the time we lived in the cabin, a grim reminder of a day of narrow escapes.

But the day did have its bright spot, too, for just at sundown Judge Robbins arrived, and with him he had our mail. Among advertisements and the weekly paper was a letter from friends, Roy and Ethel Topham of Burlingame. Since we now had a cabin large enough to accommodate visitors, we had invited them up for a few days. The letter Judge Robbins brought informed us they were coming, and would be in Downieville Saturday morning.

It was a gala occasion, for Roy and Ethel were among our oldest friends, and they would be our first real visitors. Judge Robbins stayed a while, sitting on the porch with us, relaying the latest community news. However, when the judge left, we stayed up late that night making plans for the arrival of Roy and Ethel.

For me, there still was wood to cut and fish to catch, for Roy and Ethel dearly loved fresh trout. Dot planned to spend the next day baking and readying the cabin for company. Plans also involved a shopping trip to town, and unless we could borrow a spare bed from Tony Lavazolla, a couple of people were going to have to sleep on the floor.

But, as usual, Tony came through, and not only had he a folding metal camp bed and mattress to loan us, he insisted that if this did not prove comfortable enough for our visitors, that they stay without expense at his hotel.

But as usual when I became engaged in conversation with Tony the subject eventually turned to mining. Tony wanted to know, of course, how we were doing with our sluicing on the river, and he agreed that our average of three dollars a day was considerably better than most of the snipers were doing.

"Truth is," said Tony, "most of those damn fools are wasting their time scrounging around the Hungry Mouth Gulch slide, looking for big chunks of quartz gold it might have spilled. For every piece that's been found, there's been one helluva lot of time wasted. Most of them would do better making a dollar a day with a sluice box on the river."

But Tony did admit that some fine pieces of specimen gold had been found in the slide area, and he showed us several he had bought from the snipers who had found them. One piece, shaped like a crescent, was half gold and half white quartz. The gold weighed at least a dozen ounces.

"Now, I know you're doing all right there on the river where you are," said Tony, "but I'll tell you this. There's better places than where you're working, if you want to make the effort to work them. There's an old mine up the river five or six miles, just a little coyote hole, really, that was worked around the turn of the century, and it was real rich. It was an old underground gravel channel—an old riverbed—and I was only a kid when it closed down. I saw some of the gold that came out of there—pieces the size of watermelon seeds—and one single car of ore averaged better than a thousand dollars.

"I'm not kidding you," said Tony, "I'm dead serious, Jess. That little mine was rich. Now, I'm not damn fool enough to think they didn't pretty well work it out—and neither are you. They didn't leave any of that thousand dollar-a-car gravel lying around. But, what they did do, according to the old-timers, they left a couple of pillars of pretty good gravel when they finally closed down. As far as I know they are still there."

The pillars Tony spoke of were nothing more than areas of gravel which the miners did not remove, leaving them as supports to help hold up the roof of the underground excavation, much as a center post is used to help support the ceiling of a large hall. It is no great trick to take out pillars which have been left in old mine workings like that, and it is true that many a man has made some pretty good money in such an operation.

Of course there was one thing Tony did not emphasize, the fact that the mine had not operated for some forty years. I mentioned this, plus the fact that while I certainly was not adverse to hard work or even a certain amount of danger, I preferred to do my hard work and face my danger above ground. I have never cared for underground mining.

"Oh, it was mostly all bedrock tunnel until it broke into the actual old river channel. It might be a little bit caved, and you might hit a little loose ground, but I don't think it would be too dangerous or too tough a job getting back in there," commented Tony.

We talked a bit longer about the old mine, and when Dot returned from shopping, she and I headed back to the cabin. Roy and Ethel arrived the next day, and for the time being, at least, thought of the old mine and its possible pay dirt were forgotten.

CHAPTER XI

EVERYONE FOUGHT FIRE

As I HAD DONE EACH MORNING SINCE EARLY SUMMER, I AWAKENED just as daylight was beginning to brighten the eastern horizon.

In June we had begun arising at daybreak in order to be on the river by sun-up and complete eight or nine hours of mining before the heat of mid-afternoon.

And, even before I rolled from the warm bed and put my bare feet on the worn planking of the cabin floor, I became aware of the sharp odor of smoke hanging in the still morning air.

Although it was early September and the sun was not yet topping the timbered crests of the far ridges, the air was warm and heavy with the heat of summer. Only the faintest breeze rustled the leaves of the black oaks in the cabin yard.

Dot still was sleeping, her soft breathing undisturbed by my movements as I pulled on the same shirt and tattered Levis I had worn yesterday. Ladybug raised her head from her cardboard box bed to gaze at me reproachfully for awakening her, then stood up and slowly stretched, preparing herself for our morning stroll to the outdoor privy.

With the little terrier by my side I walked slowly along the well defined path, scanning the sky for any distant plume of rising smoke. From its odor, I knew the smoke was from a brush fire, but it was difficult to determine how far away it might be. I could see no smoke column on the skyline and although I was certainly interested in the whereabouts of the blaze, at the moment I was not particularly worried. From long experience I knew that smoke from a wildfire, following the canyon air currents, could drift for miles.

When I arrived back at the cabin Dot was up and dressed and the rattle of stove lids told me she was kindling our breakfast fire.

"Gee, it sure does smell smoky," she remarked, and there was a trace of worry in her voice as she spoke.

"Yeah, we got a fire burning somewhere, all right, but it's probably quite a ways from here," I said, as I stood in the open doorway rolling a cigarette. "Smoke from a brush fire will hang close to the ground and travel quite a distance at night."

Soon the smell of frying bacon and pancakes overcame the odor of smoke from the distant fire. With breakfast finished, Dot washed the dishes while I loaded into a canvas pack sack a few mining tools we would need that day and then started to sharpen an axe.

I was just putting the finishing touches on the axe blade when Dot came to the door, a look of concern on her face.

"I think it's smokier now than it was before breakfast," she said. "Do you think we should go to work or stay here at the cabin until we find out more about this fire?"

There was no question that the smoke now was heavier than when we had awakened. Carefully, we scanned the ridge tops again but could see no tell-tale column of smoke.

"Oh, I think we're all right. This smoke is probably just drift from a fire that could be in the next county. The smoke's just building up here in the heavy air in this river canyon because there's not much wind to push it.

"Let's go on down to our diggin's. If things get to looking worse, we can always come back."

We were mining more than a mile downstream from our cabin and our path would take us past the cabin and mine of Ned Gilbert.

Gilbert was no depression day miner. He had been born

here in Sierra County some fifty years ago and had mined here all his life. His cabin sat in a little dry meadow in a bend of the river. At the head of the meadow he had driven a tunnel into the hillside and tapped an ancient, gold bearing underground river channel. He worked the mine by himself, apparently making a fair living.

As we neared Gilbert's cabin I noticed the breeze, which had barely been moving the leaves when we left our camp, seemed to have picked up a bit.

"Let's stop and see old Ned for a minute," I suggested. "He's been here a helluva lot longer and seen a lot more fires in this country than we have."

The cabin door was open and Gilbert was washing his breakfast dishes in a fire-blackened metal pan as we approached his doorstep.

"Good morning, Ned," I called out. "Kinda looks like maybe there's a fire not too far away."

Gilbert was a tall, spare man, whose body has been reduced through years of hard work to little except bone and sinew. His hands and face were tanned by sun and wind to the consistency of leather.

His most outstanding feature was a pair of black, piercing eyes and a thin, jutting nose that gave him an appearance of serious intensity. He was not a man of great humor.

He held in low regard the lately arrived hard-luck prospectors who existed in their meager camps along the river and barely tolerated the more permanent miners such as Dot and me.

Dishrag and frying pan in hand, Gilbert came to the door.

"Pretty smoky, all right," he replied. "One a'them danged fool scissorbill campers probably let a campfire get away. Burn up the whole damned country just cuz some fool city dude ain't got brains enough to throw a bucket of water on his fire."

A scarred, summer thin yellow tomcat suddenly made his

appearance in the open doorway and, with an arched back, rubbed patronizingly against Gilbert's leg. Preoccupied now with the prospects of fire, Gilbert absentmindedly pushed the cat away with his foot, stepped onto the porch and slowly scanned the skyline.

"I don't see no smoke rising, so probably that fire's pretty far off. And, it it is, I ain't gonna go looking for it."

But, as Gilbert spoke, the breeze continued to sharply rattle the leaves of surrounding trees.

"I'm kind of worred about this wind," I replied.

"Well, standing here jawing ain't gonna stop the wind from blowing . . . Looks like you fellows is on your way down to your workings, and fire or no fire, a man's gotta make a living. So, I guess I better finish these dishes and head over to my diggings."

With that, Gilbert abruptly broke off the conversation and strode back into his cabin, the scrawny yellow cat at his heels.

The first rays of morning sunlight, dull amber in the smoke-filled air, were touching the ridge tops when, ten minutes later, we turned off the main river trail into the narrow tributary ravine where we had been mining for several weeks.

The steep rock walls of this little canyon were almost vertical in places, and even in summer, the sun seldom reached its streambed. Here water trickled along the creek bottom and stood in clear pools, even during the hottest summers. In many places the ravine floor was not twenty feet wide. Ferns and other shade loving plants blanketed its walls, and here and there along its twisting course, winter storm waters had deposited beds of gold-bearing gravel.

The old timers had mined this creek long ago, but still each year, after the winter rains, it continued to yield bits of fine gold and now and then a tiny nugget. We had been averaging between two and three dollars per day, which was not too bad a wage for gold prospecting during those hungry, depression years.

A couple of pulls on its starting cord brought the little gasoline engine powered pump to life, and water from a nearby pool began flowing through our sluice box.

My shovel skimmed the shallow bedrock, feeding a constant supply of gravel into the box while, with a small rake, Dot kept it flowing evenly along the riffles and removed the larger stones.

Deep in that rock-walled little canyon we felt almost cut off from the rest of the world.

As we worked, taking notice only of the tiny grains of yellow metal accumulating in the screen riffles at the head of the sluice box, we gradually forgot the threat of fire.

But, about 10 A.M., as I paused to refill the engine, I realized that during the past three hours the fire situation had undergone drastic change.

Now, the air was rank with the odor of burning pine needles and leaves, and the sunlight that at 7 A.M. had been only slightly discolored with drifting smoke, now was yellowish brown. The smoke was so heavy it virtually blotted out all shadows.

Even deep in our narrow little ravine we could feel the rising wind, blowing directly from the north, gusting and swirling.

We wasted no time on idle discussion. I grabbed my shovel and with Dot at my heels, started down the creek.

A pall of smoke bathed the Yuba River canyon in an eerie, unreal light as though the sun was undergoing an eclipse. The smoke was so thick that we could only faintly see the eastern slope of the canyon. The wind was blowing so briskly that here and there it was kicking up small dust devils.

But, through the dense smoke, a glance to the north told us the real story.

There, across the horizon arose a broad, billowing column of black smoke.

The fire was several miles away, but even at that distance

we imagined that at its base we could see the angry glow of flames.

It required little imagination to determine what was happening. Pushed by the blustery September wind, the fire was moving down canyon—directly toward Downieville and our cabin and the miners' camps scattered along the river.

Within minutes we were at Gilbert's cabin. Old Ned was standing on the porch. He was clearly agitated. "If you fellas hadn't shown up I was gonna go down there to get you. That fire is coming down the canyon like a herd of horses. We better get into town, 'cuz I think they're gonna need everybody they can get."

Gilbert grabbed a shovel which was leaning against his cabin and led the way up the trail at a brisk pace.

Normally, it took Dot and me about twenty minutes to walk from Gilbert's to our cabin, but now, prodded by urgency, Gilbert lengthened his stride, almost forcing us to trot to keep pace with him.

Ten minutes later, gasping for breath, we arrived at our cabin. I ran over to the old Chevy and turned the key. Thankfully, it started on the first crank.

Smoke from the fire now was perceptibly heavier. We could feel its acrid sting in throat and nostrils—almost taste the scent of burning leaves and vegetation.

And, to add to our worries about the safety of the cabin, burned leaves and cinders, carried from the fire by the wind, were falling around us.

Wistfully, I looked back at our weathered little dwelling standing lonely and forlorn among the scattering of black oaks overlooking the river, and silently prayed it would still be there when we returned.

Without question, all three of us would have much preferred to remain on the river to protect our own properties, but to have done so in the face of the general threat to the community would have branded us as untrustworthy.

We had hardly reached the main road when we came upon Jim Buckman, a sniper who was camped upstream from us, headed for town at a trot with a shovel on his shoulder. We loaded him in and before we had traveled the remaining three miles to Downieville, we added two more miners to our crew. We arriced in town to find Main Street and the entire river canyon shrouded in a pall of smoke so dense that people were coughing. Visibility was reduced to only a few hundred yards.

But, as usual, the fire was farther away than it appeared. ;I stopped in front of the St. Charles Hotel where a group of men were gathered around a couple of uniformed U.S. Forest Service officials.

The fire, we quickly learned, was burning toward town from Saddleback Mountain and around the Craycroft Diggings and Empire Creek, some three miles to the north.

But, with the wind pushing it, three miles was not far.

Merchants and townspeople, including women and older children, were filling tubs, barrels, wash boilers and buckets with water to wet down roofs or fight flames if the fire reached town. They worked with the intense purposefulness that defenders of medieval castles once must have employed, for this town too, at the moment, was under siege.

Some of the women had gathered up their younger children and taken them to the school, where several older matrons were riding herd on them like agitated mother hens.

A forest service road crew foreman and his men had been pulled in from their road job near Camptonville. They loaded me, the four men I had brought in, and several others into a pickup truck and we headed for the fire. As we drove away, I looked back and saw my wife walking toward Tony Lavazolla's hotel.

We were headed up the ridge where, a couple miles from town, fire fighters already on the scene were clearing a line from which we could backfire.

But, just at the edge of town, as we started up the hill, the driver of an old iron-tired tractor with a plow hitched to it was trying to cut a fireline around the face of the slope. The plow bucked and lurched, hardly more than scratching the rocky soil which was hard and dry after a long, rainless summer. He was assisted by several older men. Some worked with shovels while others carried bundles of burlap grain sacks which they soaked in the nearby creek. This, in case the fireline farther up the ridge failed, would be the town's last line of defense. The wet sacks, if necessary, would be used to beat out flames advancing through the grass.

As we neared the fire, the smoke and heat increased by the moment.

Our fifteen-minute trip ended in a small, natural basin across the bottom of which sprawled corrals, a barn, several out-buildings and a weatherbeaten, gray two-story house. Several men were wetting down the roofs of the barn and other buildings with buckets of water, and a woman was spraying the house with a hose.

Our driver parked his truck beside a cluster of vehicles and turned us over to a smoke-grimed fire boss whose shirt already had several holes burned in it by falling cinders. He led us off at a trot up a hillside covered with pine needles and clumps of mountain misery overlooking the valley that contained the ranch.

"I'm sure glad to see you fellows," he gasped. "We gotta get a line around this hill so we can backfire from it and we haven't got enough men. There's a forest service bulldozer coming in from Camptonville, but I don't think it will get here in time."

We spread out along the hillside, scraping down to bare earth a two-foot-wide swath from which we would safely be able to start the backfire which we hoped would stop the advancing wildfire.

Although the main fire had not yet topped the ridge above us, the wind was driving its heat and smoke ahead of it in a withering blast that made us cough and gasp for breath.

The whole world seemed to have sunken into a half-light. It was only early afternoon, but the sun was a dull, coppery glow in the sky, virtually obliterated by the vast wall of smoke. The wind continued unabated, and our shirts already were sweat-soaked from the heat and exertion.

I had traded my shovel for a McLeod, a heavy, hoe-like tool that I had grabbed out of a forest service truck. Its broad, sharp blade was far superior to a shovel for scraping and clearing ground.

Suddenly, it was mid-afternoon and if possible, the smoke was even heavier. Sweat ran down my forehead and stung my eyes. Bits of cinder and blackened leaves which had been falling for some time were falling more heavily, and some still were smoking when they landed. Although they started no fires, we often had to run quickly to stamp out the larger ones that fell behind our line.

It was hot, exhausting work, but when I straightened up to catch my breath for a moment and looked across the hillside, it appeared that our fireline was complete. Off to my left some thirty yards Ned Gilbert straightened up, swatted at a burning ember which had landed on the back of his shirt and took notice of our accomplishment.

"By God . . . I think we've got her hooked."

But there was no time for celebrating.

We didn't really see the flames as much as we sensed and heard them. The fire hit the top of the ridge a quarter-mile to the north of our fireline with a seething, crackling roar.

Long tongues of flame climbed a hundred feet into the air and heavy black smoke from the thick stands of second growth timber that were burning torchlike came rolling in great, billowing whorls ahead of the fire.

The wind seemed to sweep down on us with blast furnace heat; the air was filled with burning debris that blistered the skin and set individual blazes when it fell in dry grass or pine needles. Spot fires already were breaking out at the edge of the timber line, ahead of the main blaze.

From these spot fires long fingers of flame went streaking wickedly before the wind, cutting through the patches of mountain misery and squaw carpet.

Cringing against the heat, we pulled our shirt collars up to at least partially protect necks and faces and constantly slapped at the red hot cinders which landed on us.

Then, along our fire break men were running. The smoke had become so thick we heard them before we actually saw them. Our fire boss, a burning fuse in hand, with two other forest service men, was leaning down to touch off the grass and pine needles and start our backfire.

Another tall, leathery faced crew foreman, his dark green shirt now blackened by sweat, came running up with a broom he had dipped in kerosene. He ran along our section of the fireline, dragging the flaming broom, and fire leaped up behind it.

He ran along the line until the kerosene flames on the broom built up so high the wind whipped them back into his face, then he hurled its burning remains far beyond the line into the pine needles which again instantly ignited.

Pinned down by the wind blowing against it, the backfire in many places sputtered, but its grass and pine needle fuel, tinder dry, kept it alive, although at first the flames moved slowly.

All along the line, fire fighters, their eyes smarting and watering from the heat and acrid smoke, cursed the backfire's inactivity. A couple of men actually ran through the low flames of the backfire to start other blazes closer to the main fire, but they traveled only a few yards before the searing heat of the main blaze, only a few hundreds yards away, drove them back.

Then, as so often happens in the foothills, the wind swirled and eddied, and for a moment a gust actually blew toward the north, pushing our backfire into the face of the oncoming blaze.

Aided by the momentary wind change, the backfire came to life. Suddenly, its flames were shooting high into the air and it was racing up the slope toward the main fire.

As the fires drew together, the steadily advancing backfire was sucked up in the draft created by the main blaze. With an eerie hiss that swelled into a deep-throated roar, the two walls of fire met, and a swirling hurricane of flame leaped hundreds of feet into the air, engulfing whole pine trees.

The fire was so hot that all along the hillside between our fireline and the main fire, individual pine trees that had not burned when the backfire swept beneath them began bursting into flame. Each tree, as the heat ignited it, flared for a minute or two into a towering yellow torch that died down to leave the tips of its denuded boughs glowing bright red. Moments later, it was only a blackened skeleton against the smoke-filled sky.

A hundred feet in front of me an eighty-foot Ponderosa pine, its branches whipping in the terrible updraft of heat, exploded like a Roman candle, spewing burning bark and needles high into the air.

Cringing from the heat, I bent low to the ground to protect my face. Sparks were falling everywhere and spot fires were breaking out on our side of the line. By the time I reached the nearest one it already had burned an area a yard square, but the grass and pine needles were fairly sparse, and in a moment I had it controlled. Other men all along the line also were beating out spot fires.

Behind us, suddenly, over the noise of wind and fire there were shouts, and at the old ranch in the basin at the bottom of the slope, the barn and several sheds were ablaze. An instant later, fire also burst out on the weathered shake roof of the old ranchhouse.

Futilely, a man who had climbed onto the roof sprayed it with the garden hose, but the flames only leaped higher.

Others dowsed the walls with buckets of water without noticeable effect.

"Stay here! . . . Stay here and watch the fireline, or we'll lose everything," shouted our fire boss, as we turned to run toward the burning buildings.

"We can't save that house now," he said, "and if we go down there the fire will jump this line."

We knew he was right, even though it seemed hard-hearted not to at least lend a hand at trying to save the old dwelling.

One of the forest service men did take several fire fighters down the hill to the old ranch, but not to help put out the fires in the buildings. Instead, they quickly began building a fireline around the buildings to keep the fire from spreading into the surrounding woods and fields.

And, still of major concern were several spots along the eastern end of our line where heavy clumps of small pines and firs still were burning, and we had to hope the line would hold.

In fact, there were places on the far end of the line, a half-mile up the ridge from us, where sections of the fireline had not yet been tied together and from which they had not been able to backfire.

"Come on, boys, let's go give those fellows a hand," yelled another of our fire bosses.

We could see heavy smoke rolling up from around the point of the ridge, and we knew there was real danger there of the fire getting away, but it also seemed doubtful at that moment if our handful of exhausted men would be able to stop the fire.

I was running along with several others toward the new area of fire danger when, from the timber at the edge of the little valley below us, emerged a line of men moving along at a trot.

Each carried a shovel or McLeod, and several had water-filled pack pumps strapped on their backs.

They were Civilian Conservation Corpsmen from the camp in Indian Valley, and I never in my life was more glad to see anyone.

The CCC boys broke into two groups. The smaller group

ran to the burning house and began helping move furniture from it. The remainder, more than a dozen young men, came running up the hill and headed for the far end of the line where the fire still was threatening.

With their pack-pumps they knocked down the spot fires and with shovels and McLeods began linking together the last segments of the fireline.

Then, suddenly, in our sector at least, the main danger was over.

Hit by the backfire, the advancing flames of the main fire, robbed of their fuel supply, blazed up in spiraling ribbons that quickly dissipated into a meteor shower of sparks and writhing columns of black smoke.

The roar of the fire that at times had seemed to shake the earth also suddenly was gone. The silence that followed seemed almost weird.

And, for the first time that day, it seemed, I paused to catch my breath and roll a cigarette. The fire danger had ended here, and as I picked up a smouldering twig to light my cigarette, I suddenly realized that the lack of light was not all caused by the pall of smoke from the fire.

It already was well past sundown and dusk was rapidly creeping up on us. With the coming of evening, the wind also had begun to drop, and the branches of the trees were scarcely moving.

The silence was broken only by the soft mumble of conversation here and there along the fireline, or by an occasional shout off somewhere in the distance.

Smoke still hung heavy in the air, and below us in the little valley, the old farmhouse, barn and most of the other buildings were charred ruins. Only the ranch corrals of peeled, weather-whitened fir poles remained intact.

Around the smoking remains of the old dwelling, among remnants of furniture that had been saved, several people, at least some of them women, moved about in the gathering darkness.

There was little to do except keep watch for an occasional spark that might drift across the line, and as I relaxed there, our fire boss, followed by several CCC boys, came striding down the line.

With him also were several of our volunteer fire crew, including Ned Gilbert, who had been fighting the blaze since early in the day.

"Come on, Java old boy," said the foreman. "These Three-Cee Boys are going to take over for a while and let us get something to eat. They tell me some women have come up from town and have set up a kitchen back there at the cross-roads and are feeding fire fighters. Let's get down there before it's all gone."

We started down the hill, and as I tossed my McLeod into the bed of one of the forestry trucks parked there in the basin, I suddenly realized it had been twelve hours since I had eaten. I also was dog tired.

In darkness, we stumbled along the rutted, dusty road until far in the distance, we could see the glow of Coleman lanterns and automobile headlights.

There in a little glade at the intersection of two old woods roads, smoke-grimed fire fighters milled about in front of a couple of makeshift tables from which several women, under the direction of Tony Lavazolla, were dishing up hot food.

And suddenly I realized that the woman with a red bandanna tied around her hair, who was ladling out big scoops of beans, was my wife.

"Hi," she called out from across the table as she caught sight of me. "I see you made it back . . . You look kinda beat, and, my God!—look at your shirt—you must have a million holes burned in it!"

For the first time, I paused to take stock of myself, and despite Dot's considerable exaggeration, I had to admit there were more holes than there was shirt left on my back.

When they finished serving us, Dot came around the table and sat beside me on the log where I was eating.

"I haven't been exactly sitting still since I left you at the hotel this morning," she said. "I had no more than got inside the door when Tony grabbed me and sent me shopping for food. He said the fire crews would have to be fed and there was no telling when the forest service might get around to doing it, so the job was up to us. I've been peeling potatoes and onions and cooking pots of beans, and this is the third place we've gone to feed fire fighters today. Tony says that now we've got to take food to a crew up the canyon a ways."

I also learned from Dot, who had been talking to fire crews and fire bosses from several areas, that the fire still was out of control both up-canyon and down-canyon from town. We had stopped the fire at its center, but it now was burning around at both ends.

However, she added, there were reports that a bulldozer had arrived and now was getting a line around the down-river end of the fire.

"But they say that some cabins and camps down the river in our direction have been burned, and I'm just sick worrying that maybe our cabin was one of them."

There was no time for further talk.

A forest ranger arrived and within minutes we were in trucks, headed up the highway toward Sierra City. For the remainder of the night we cut firelines and fought hot spots, but toward morning as the air grew heavier, the fire cooled.

Shortly before noon we were relieved by a fresh crew from Nevada City, and at mid-afternoon, with the fire generally under control, a uniformed forest service man told us volunteers we could go home.

I found Dot still working in the hotel kitchen. She also had been without sleep for thirty-six hours, and she, too, was ready to call it quits.

Dot retrieved Ladybug from the hotel room where she had been confined for most of her stay in town, and I rounded up Ned Gilbert, who said he had all the fire fighting he needed for the year.

"I'd have done some shopping before we left town," said Dot, "but there isn't much left in the store to buy. In order to feed you fire fighters we just about cleaned out the store. I don't think there's a loaf of bread in town."

We passed several spots where fire had burned to the edge of the highway before it was stopped, but soon we were what appeared to be beyond the area of the blaze.

With a sigh of relief I turned the Chevy onto our own winding road and a few moments later saw our cabin standing unharmed, just as we had left it, on the tree-shaded point overlooking the river.

We were rejoicing along with Ned Gilbert when we happened to glance downstream and suddenly noticed in the still smoky air that smoke was rising from a point a helf-mile or so downstream.

"Why, by damn," said Gilbert, "that there fire has burned around this area and went on down there around my place. I better get down there and see what happened."

"Wait a minute," I told him. "I'm going with you."

We didn't really run all the way down there, but for two tired men, we covered that mile of river trail awfully fast.

The last half mile was over burned land, where brush, stumps and half-burned debris still smouldered. We both knew what we were likely to find, but would not allow ourselves to believe it until we rounded the last turn of the river.

Gilbert, who was in the lead, stopped.

Where his cabin has stood there was only a half-fallen chimney and a pile of charred rubble.

Slowly, we walked the remaining hundred yards to stand wordlessly beside the still smoking pile of charred boards and ashes.

Oddly enough, although the cabin had burned to the ground, Gilbert's combination woodshed and blacksmith shop, where he sharpened and repaired his mining tools, had not burned.

As we stood there viewing the loss, the skinny yellow tomcat, hair slightly singed, emerged from an unburned clump of bushes and, approaching without fear, arched his back and rubbed against Gilbert's ankle.

Gilbert looked down at the scrawny old cat, a wry expression on his face. "Poor old sonuvagun—you ain't got much home left, have you?"

Then, in a more serious vein, he added, "Hell, it ain't too bad. Nothing was there that can't be replaced or rebuilt, and for the time being, I can make out in that woodshed if I can gt ahold of a frying pan and a couple of blankets."

For the next few days, over his protests, old Ned stayed with Dot and me while he gathered together enough to live for a while in his revamped woodshed. He made daily trips down to his camp to feed the old cat.

A month later, on a Sunday morning, a lumber truck stopped on the highway above Ned Gilbert's camp. With it were Dot and me and several people from town, including old Jack and Tony Lavazolla and a half dozen snipers from along the river.

We unloaded the lumber and skidded it down the hill to the little flat where Gilbert's mine was located.

That night before the sun had set a quite respectable little cabin, complete with stove, table, chairs and bed stood on the exact spot where old Ned's original cabin had stood. Ned had supplied the lumber; we supplied the labor.

Even the old yellow cat liked the new cabin.

CHAPTER XII

HAPPENING ON THE YUBA

ROY AND ETHEL TOOK A SINGLE LOOK AT OUR CABIN ON THE BLUFF above the river and offered to trade places with us, hands down. They marveled at the mountains and the scenery, filled their lungs with clean, pine-scented air, and relaxed in wilderness silence broken only by sound of the river or occasional scolding of a distant squirrel or bluejay.

"I can see why you haven't come back to San Jose—if I had a place like this you couldn't chase me away from it or pay me enough to come back to the city," Roy commented expansively.

We idled away the afternoon on the broad, pine-shaded cabin porch, recapping old times and caught up on events that made either Roy or Ethel believe we had not been on a continuous three-year vacation, that just making a living here had been and still was a tough day-to-day situation.

"But, you look so tanned, so relaxed, so self-sufficient, and healthy," commented Ethel.

Around 4 P.M. Dot stood up, stretched, and announced that if we were going to have trout for dinner she knew a couple of fellows that had better get busy catching them. I took down my long fishing rod that hung on a couple of nails on the side of the cabin. From its storage place beneath the porch I collected a piece of window screen about three feet long and two feet wide. Each end of the screen was tacked to a stick so the screen could be stretched and held rigid.

"Come on, Roy," I said, "let's go catch our dinner."

Roy look questioningly at the piece of screen.

"Just exactly what do you propose to do with that screen? Do you plan to try and net the trout with it?"

"No," I told him. "I'll stick to the rod when it comes to catching fish, but we'll get our bait with this screen." Roy looked puzzled.

"You planning on catching grasshoppers?"

We walked down the slope to the river, and choosing a shallow section of rapids, I told Roy to spread the screen and hold it across the current to catch anything that would wash against it. I moved upstream from the screen a yard or so and began turning over rocks with my hands. I rolled a couple dozen cantaloupe-sized rocks, then told Roy to lift the screen.

Caught on the upstream side of the screen were a dozen inch-long hellgramites, aquatic larvae of the stone fly which make up one of the staple trout foods of western Sierra streams. Three more sweeps and we had more than thirty hellgramites squirming in the bottom of an old Prince Albert tobacco can I used as a bait container. Roy was no outdoorsman and certainly no fisherman. This was all new to him.

"Well," he commented dryly, "even if you don't catch any fish maybe we can at least eat the bait."

"Don't laugh," I replied. "The Indians used to catch hellgramites and roast and eat them just as they did grasshoppers."

"I'll bet they didn't catch them with chunks of window screen," was Roy's only comment.

Late-afternoon shadows were falling across the stream as we moved up to a long, deep pool where the current swirled slowly into a wide eddy.

Deep in the clear water we could see pan-sized trout working in the edge of the swifter current. Every few moments one would dart forward to grab some morsel which was being swept past him. Carefully, I impaled a hellgramite on a No. 8 bait hook and cast it into the pool, across and upstream from where the trout were feeding.

The bait landed almost in midstream, swung into the current, and sank slightly below the surface as it traveled down toward the waiting trout. An instant later, although I had noticed no particular movement in the pool, I felt the slightest tug on my line and it suddenly began moving across current.

I set the hook, my homemade willow rod arched. A nine-inch rainbow trout danced to the surface and did a complete flip in an effort to free himself. An instant later I was stowing the still wriggling fish into the flour sack which served as my creel.

In little more than an hour I had fished a half-dozen pools and in my creel were twenty-five trout, from seven inches to nearly a foot long to add to our dinner menu. We cleaned and washed them in the ice-cold stream and arrived back at the cabin a half hour before the last rays of sunshine left the ridgetops above us. Dot already had a fire going in the cabin wood stove, and the odor of woodsmoke and slight chill of evening whetted our appetites.

Twenty-five trout, which was the legal limit during the 1930s, may seem like quite a few for just four people at a single meal. But by the time supper was over and we were sipping a last cup of coffee, the entire catch had been reduced to a pile of bones.

We sat up late that night, talking, drinking coffee, and watching the outdoor fire I had built to take the chill off the night air. Midnight arrived before we finally went to bed, driven off the porch and indoors by the increasing cold. It was wonderful having Roy and Ethel there—like a vacation for Dot and me. And for the first time in many weeks we would be able to sleep late in the morning.

But morning came and I, at least, did not sleep late. Shortly after daylight that damned gray squirrel was at the window clamoring for his breakfast. Finally, in self-defense I got up and fed him. I crawled back into bed where Dot was still sleeping soundly, but used to arising early, I found that once awake I could not go back to sleep. While everyone else snored, I got up, dressed, put the coffee on to boil and went fishing.

By the time the rest of my crew was up and dressed I was back with another limit of trout for breakfast. We planned no work during the three days Roy and Ethel were to stay with us, and after breakfast we decided to take them for a ride to show them the Downieville country. Roy was interested in mines and mining, and suddenly I remembered the old gravel mine Tony Lavazolla had told me about.

"How would you like to explore a real underground mine—an old-timer that produced rich pay in the early days and is still supposed to have some good spots in it . . ." I asked Roy. Naturally, Roy was all for the idea. While the girls put together a picnic lunch I rummaged through my belongings and came up with a miner's carbide lamp. Roy had a flashlight in his car which he planned to use.

In addition to the carbide lamp I also took a prospector's pick, a small, short-handled shovel, and a couple of small canvas bags to use as sample sacks.

We stopped in Downieville to talk to Tony and get specific directions on how to find the old mine. While we talked, Roy, Ethel, and Dot each drank a glass of sherry, but in those days, being a teetotaler, I abstained. As usual I took a pretty good kidding about being a bluenose.

The mine, said Tony, should not be difficult to find, since an old road led to it, and the remains of a couple of mine buildings should still be standing near the tunnel entrance. Carefully, he drew us a map.

We parked the car at the intersection of a county road and the old mine road which long ago had been abandoned to all but foot traffic. Fair-sized pine trees grew in the roadway which once had been used by wagons, and lush fern and pink wildflowers hung over the roadbank. The road lay on the shady side of the hill and the grass still was green in the open glades among the pine trees. In the openings bloomed wildflowers.

A small pine, bent by winter snows, leaned across our path. As we stooped to pass beneath it a frightened mother robin burst from her nest in the tree, inches above our heads.

A fifteen-minute walk brought us to the mine, and Tony had not exaggerated when he estimated it had not operated for forty years. The buildings he spoke of were only crushed ruins of rotting boards, having long ago succumbed to the ravages of time and winter snows. The mine tunnel itself was not difficult to find, for the old mine dump, a huge pile of round, alluvial boulders, still was quite apparent. A tiny stream of cold, clear water flowed from the mouth of the tunnel, with green grass growing along its edges.

The mouth of the tunnel, even though blasted into hard bedrock, was partially caved and covered over by soil which over the years had sluffed down the hill. However, preliminary examination indicated the tunnel walls solid and safe enough for us to enter it. One thing was sure, with the amount of water running from the tunnel mouth, I knew we were going to get plenty wet and muddy before we got out of there.

I looked at Roy, who was carrying his flashlight and peering into the darkness of the old tunnel.

"You still want to go in there?"

Roy gulped a bit, and I could see his enthusiasm for gold-mine exploration had waned considerably since breakfast time, but he still was game. He gave me a somewhat sickly grin.

"Sure, let's go," he said, clutching his flashlight and sounding considerably braver than he probably felt.

"Don't you want to eat before you go poking around in that old mine?" asked Dot, as she took the lunch basket which I had been carrying.

"No, we won't be gone long—just want to look around inside a bit and take a few samples of the gravel left in those pillars," I replied. "We might as well get it over with now, and then we'll have the whole afternoon to show Roy and Ethel the rest of the country."

I filled the carbide lamp, lit it, and with a final wave to the girls Roy and I entered the tunnel. For the first few yards we picked our way over broken rock, and pieces of old, rotted mine timber, but soon we were in a clear area where the hard rock walls and roof seemed more solid. The tunnel was fair sized, about six feet wide and seven feet high. A flow of cold water perhaps an inch deep trickled along the low side of the floor and formed small pools in places where debris dammed it up.

My carbide light and Roy's flashlight bit into the darkness ahead of us. We still could look over our shoulders and see daylight framed in the mouth of the tunnel, and it gave us a feeling of safety. We could feel the old, rusted mine car rails and their rotting wooden ties beneath our feet, but the going was easy and we traveled at a fast walk. The air was cool and carried the musty smell of decayed wood.

For some two hundred yards we walked straight into the tunnel, and, as Tony had predicted, the tunnel itself had withstood the years well. Then, it turned sharply to the left and darkness seemed to become more dense—to close in on us—and we could no longer see the friendly spot of daylight at the tunnel mouth. For a long distance the floor of the tunnel followed an even, almost flat grade, but some yards after we rounded a second curve we suddenly hit a sharp incline.

The solid bedrock walls of the tunnel gave way to piles of broken rock and round boulders such as are found along stream beds and river channels. The walls of the tunnel widened, but suddenly it lost height, and we were reduced to crawling on hands and knees in some places. Loose rock had fallen, and over the years had filled this section of passageway until it was little more than a coyote hole about three feet high.

Behind the fallen rock water had welled up to a depth of a couple feet. It was ice cold and so clear the light from my carbide lamp cut through it to sharply define the rocks in the bottom of the pool. I tested the water for depth, plunging one arm to the bottom, for it was so transparent it was difficult to tell how deep it really was. Then, gritting my teeth, I waded through. Behind me I heard Roy suck in his breath sharply as he stepped into it: "Damn, that water's cold!"

The excavation or stope—it could no longer truly be called a tunnel—widened again, but the rock roof was close over our heads. Fallen rock and rubble were everywhere. The beams of our lights darted here and there, picking up fallen and rotten timbers, a rusted, broken shovel, and what appeared to be a half-buried ore car.

Everything we touched or crawled over now was wet and coated with a yellow, clayish mud. I looked back at Roy and his face and clothes were smeared with it. I couldn't help laughing, even though I knew I probably looked as bad or worse.

"Roy, the only way you could be wetter or muddier is to be bigger," I told him.

"Well, Jess, you don't look exactly like a fashion model yourself." We crawled another dozen boulder-strewn yards.

Then, Roy spoke up again. "Say, Jess . . . I don't think I really want to go any farther in here. I am getting awfully dirty, and I'm not used to this sort of thing . . ."

"OK, Roy," I told him. "I don't think there's much use of going any farther anyway. This all looks pretty badly caved in here, and I think we're wasting our time."

But, at the same time I hated to give up, now that I was here, and I knew that if there was any good ground left, it still lay ahead of us.

"Tell you what, Roy . . . You wait here for me, and I'm going to crawl on around this next bend and see what it looks like," I told him. "You stay here and I'll be back in a few minutes. I'm only going a few yards farther on."

I left Roy sitting forlornly on a pile of boulders in the old underground workings and dragging my sample sacks and prospecting pick behind me, I headed off on hands and knees, farther into the old mine. Now I was in what appeared to be center of the old underground river channel area, I could see where the early-day miners, who worked this place before I was born, had stacked and built walls with the larger excess rock as they removed the finer, gold-rich gravel.

Ahead of me the diggings appeared to fork, with the main excavation to my right, but a smaller tunnel or coyote hole bearing off to the left. I crawled on ahead, entering the left fork. It was four or five feet wide, and about three or four feet high, but after a few yards it suddenly narrowed and became lower. I crawled on a few more feet, planning to turn around and start back. Over one last pile of boulders I wriggled, and suddenly, I was sliding downward head-first in wet, slimy mud into deep water.

Somehow, I managed to keep my light from going under, and caught myself with just my head and one arm and shoulder above water. Behind me, I could hear rock falling. Several boulders came rolling down and splashed into the pool of water.

Realizing what a damned fool I had been to venture so far into this narrow trap, I started back the way I had come, slipping, sliding on mud-slick rocks as I climbed up the boulder pile. A broken, sharp-edged rock slashed the palm of my hand, and a moment later, a large rusted spike protruding from a piece of rotten timber caught my pants leg and ripped it from knee to ankle.

Now, I realized that in crawling over the top of the boulder pile I had jarred more rock loose from the roof. In falling it had partially blocked my return passage.

I did not feel I was in trouble—at least I didn't think I was—but I wondered if rather than try to return the way I had come it would not be better to keep moving on in the hope this small branch might lead back into the main diggings. Carefully, I backed down the boulder pile, half-swam half-walked through the pool of water and into the tunnel beyond it.

The floor and roof were not more than two feet apart now, and I felt a closeness I did not like. I was practically crawling on my belly now, and for the first time, I was becoming worried. If this hole I was crawling into did continue on to connect with the main part of the mine I should be able to shout and Roy would hear me, I reasoned. I shouted once, then again, but the only thing I heard was the echo of my own voice.

It was then I noticed something that I had not realized before. I was having difficulty breathing. I was not getting enough air, I felt warm, and somehow it seemed difficult to think. Remembering something that old miners had told me years before, I looked at my carbide lamp. The bright, narrow flame that normally issued from its burner had leaped away from the burner by two inches or more—an indication of lack of oxygen.

I shook my head and tried to think clearly. There was no time now for further exploration or to take a chance this passageway I was in might lead to the main tunnel. I turned around, trying not to panic, and crawled back—fast as I could—the way I had come. I reached the pool of water and the air seemed to be better. I crawled through the water and the cold shock also helped revive me. Up the boulder pile I crawled, ever so slowly it seemed, past where I had cut my hand and torn my pants. Pushing, pulling, and wriggling, I squeezed over the top of the boulders, my back sometimes scraping on the roof.

My earlier passage had disturbed loose rock which had tumbled down closing the narrow aperture over the boulder pile to a considerable degree. Even as I made my way through the narrowest part now, more rock fell. A rock which probably was no larger than my two fists, but which felt as big as a watermelon, struck me on the upper arm. But, I was breathing freely now, the carbide light was burning better, and a moment later I saw Roy's flashlight in the distance.

I reached the spot where Roy was waiting for me, and I could see even before he spoke that he was anxious.

"My Lord, Jess, where have you been? You said you were

only going a little farther and you've been gone a good forty-five minutes. I was getting pretty damned worried."

I couldn't believe I had been back in that dangerous damned cubbyhole that long—it seemed as if I had been gone only a few minutes—but a look at Roy's watch confirmed his statement. We started for the mouth of the tunnel. In less than ten minutes we reached the daylight turn and could see sunshine framed in the mouth of the tunnel. It was a comforting sight indeed.

But the greeting that Roy had given me was nothing to what Dot and Ethel said when they saw us, mud-spattered, filthy, with torn clothes, as we emerged from the mouth of the tunnel. My hand was still bleeding slightly, and somewhere in the mine I had lost my prospecting pick and sample sacks. We washed as best we could before starting on the sandwiches, but suddenly my appetite was gone. I began to realize what a close call I really had—what that bad air and caving ground could have meant. I just didn't feel much like eating.

Roy and I were so dirty and mud-stained in spite of our efforts to clean ourselves that the girls would not even allow us to stop in Downieville to tell Tony about our mine exploration. Next day, when Roy and Ethel left for San Jose, would be plenty of time to stop in Downieville, they said. Meanwhile, I already had made up my mind privately that any future mining or mine seeking that I did would be strictly above the ground.

We sent Roy and Ethel off with another limit of trout packed in ice obtained in Downieville, along with a promise they would return soon. Tony Lavazolla was out of town that day, so we didn't even get to tell him about the previous day's experience. Instead, Dot and I headed back to the cabin to get started on some serious mining of our own.

I had hit a spot of good ground, a high bench several yards from the river that was paying well. The old-timers apparently had been unable or had not taken time to get water directly on this spot. Instead, they probably had wheelbarrowed the pay dirt to a sluice box closer to the river. As a result, they had not cleaned the bedrock as well as they usually did. They also left a considerable amount of unworked gravel apparently considered too low grade to bother with, but it suited me fine.

With aid of pump and hose I could bring water directly to the bench, so I set up a full-sized sluice box—what the old-timers called a "longtom." But to clean up a longtom at the end of a day's work entails considerably more time than to clean up one of the short, little sniper's sluice boxes of the type we generally employed. I got into the habit of cleaning the longtom about every three days. We were averaging nearly five dollars per day.

A few days later as I arrived at work one morning, I noticed several footprints around the sluice box that were neither mine nor Dot's.

The prints puzzled me, but for the moment I dismissed them. I knew that other snipers often traveled up and down the river for one reason or another. More often than not, if they observed some other prospector's diggings, they would stop to take a look.

But for some reason, as I worked there that morning, memory of those footprints bothered me. There were few miners camped downriver from us. Also the river trail at this point followed the hillside some two hundred yards above my sluice box. Few persons, looking down from the trail would expend the effort to travel that steep two hundred yards just to examine what some other sniper was doing. I said nothing to Dot, who was working beside me, but at noon while she was building a fire to boil the coffee, I began lifting the sluice box riffles—the first step in cleaning it up.

By the time the coffee was boiling I had the sluice box pretty well washed down—much to Dot's surprise, for it was unusual that I cleaned up a sluice box at midday. I washed the black sand and other heavy, residual material down the sluice box into a bucket at its lower end. But even as the fine sand and gravel swept down the box I noticed an absence of the tiny flakes of gold that generally trailed behind the moving sand.

The last of the sand sloshed into the bucket and I transferred it to a gold pan which I swirled in a small nearby pool. I had not cleaned up the sluice box for two and a half days, and it should have contained at least twelve dollars in fine gold and tiny nuggets. Instead, as I stared at the now washed-down gold pan, I was looking at about two dollars' worth of gold—just about what I had mined that morning. There was no question now what those footprints around the sluice box had meant.

There was no use trying to kid Dot or hide the truth. I told her what apparently had happened. That afternoon we cleaned up the sluice box before we went home.

Having the sluice box robbed and loss of what I figured was close to fifteen dollars' worth of gold was bad enough, but what worried me was what might happen to our cabin while we were gone. We often had a week's gold sitting in a bottle on a shelf in the kitchen, and there was food and many other things of value that could be taken.

That evening after supper, now having acquired the 30-30 Winchester, I took the rifle and walked downriver to a spot which overlooked our sluice box. I sat there until long after dark but nothing happened. Each evening I repeated the routine.

Saturday morning we drove to Downieville and I quietly told Tony Lavazolla and Judge Robbins about the sluice box robbery.

"I'm not surprised," said Tony. "During the past two or three weeks I've had three or four people tell me just about the same thing. There's a sniper camped below town a mile or so who swears somebody has been fooling with his sluice box, and a couple fellows up near Hungry Mouth Gulch told the sheriff their camps were ransacked."

We agreed with Tony and the judge that all we could do was clean up our sluice boxes every day and keep any gold or valuables we had at the cabin well hidden. One problem that faced Dot and me was that our cabin was pretty well isolated. Unlike on the Agua Fria, we had no other snipers whom we knew and could trust, living near us. The only neighbor we had, and he lived nearly a half mile upstream from us, was an old man I knew only as Fred.

Old Fred was a pensioner, well up in his seventies, but he still mined when he felt good, and was reputedly an expert at the business. Fred was no Depression days or hard-times miner. He had lived on the river for years, and once, when I had stopped at his cabin on my way upriver, he had shown me some nice nuggets he had taken recently from a crevice.

Fred lived quietly in his one-room cabin on the Yuba with his little mongrel dog. If he was not mining he whiled away his days on the cabin porch, his dog asleep beside him. Once in a great while he walked down to our cabin, and a couple of times, he rode into Downieville with us in the Chevvy. Fred knew and was liked by every man and woman in the community.

A month had passed since our sluice box robbery and I had more or less forgotten about it. One Sunday morning Dot was washing clothes and I was busy cutting wood when I was attracted by the whining of a dog. I looked up, and a few yards from me stood old Fred's little black and white mongrel. At first I thought Fred probably was on his way to visit us and the dog had trotted on ahead of him. Fred did not show up, and the dog continued to trot in circles, look at me and whine.

For ten minutes or more the little dog stayed near me. Finally, Ladybug heard him, dashed out of the cabin barking furiously, and tried to chase him away. The dog ran, but came back, and Ladybug gave chase again. This time the dog disappeared and I did not see him again. Ladybug, quite self-satisfied at having driven off an intruder, went back to the cabin to gloat over her victory.

By mid-afternoon I had finished cutting wood, and after changing clothes I suggested to Dot that we take a walk up the river and visit old Fred. I was puzzled by his dog's actions.

It was around 4 P.M. when we neared Fred's cabin, which nestled in a grove of small, second-growth pine and big black oaks. Suddenly, I knew something was very wrong.

The little mongrel I had seen that morning as I was cutting wood did not come running toward us, barking as he always did when a visitor arrived. There was neither sign nor sound of activity at the cabin. No smoke issued from the chimney. I lengthened my stride, and as we drew nearer, I saw the front door of the cabin was ajar. Leaving Dot outside I pushed the door open and stepped in.

The interior of the cabin was a shambles—it had been ransacked—and old Fred lay dead in his bed. On the floor in front of the old man's bunk was his little dog. He had died defending his master. The bloody ax which had killed him had been flung into a corner.

It was almost dark by the time we returned with the sheriff and a half-dozen others who had all been friends of old Fred. Examination showed that Fred apparently had died in his sleep of natural causes. It was after he was dead someone had entered the cabin to ransack it and to do so, had been forced to kill his little dog.

Apparently the ransacking and death of the dog occurred some time after the dog had visited our cabin that morning. We found not a speck of gold in old Fred's cabin. Someone had taken it all.

Officially the robbery of my sluice box and sluice boxes of others, as well as the burglary of old Fred's cabin and killing of his dog, were never solved.

However, some weeks after old Fred's death, a sniper on the river below Goodyear's Bar left his diggings one afternoon, forgetting his tobacco pouch. After supper, wanting a smoke, he walked back to get his tobacco and surprised two men cleaning out his sluice box.

The sniper carried no gun, but a miner's shovel is a vicious weapon. He grabbed one he had left leaning against a rock near the sluice box, and moved in on the two sluice box robbers. Both men got away, but not before they lost considerable hide, and one of them left most of his teeth scattered on the ground beside the sluice box.

The pair apparently fled the country without even returning to their own camp. An abandoned camp was found a week or so later with all the equipment for two men. Among the belongings, which were turned over to the sheriff, were several ounces of gold, including a number of pretty nice-sized nuggets, and a pistol that people recognized as having belonged to old Fred.

CHAPTER XIII

SIERRA WINTER

ALMOST WITHOUT OUR REALIZING IT, SUMMER SLIPPED AWAY. Suddenly it was September and the morning air was crisp. The ranks of vacationers and campers, who all summer long had pitched their tents in the meadows and flats along the river, thinned perceptibly. Fishermen were fewer. Within a short time they would give way to deer hunters.

All summer we had mined the gravel bars along the river, averaging from one dollar to three dollars per day. But now, with the first frost only weeks away and leaves soon to be turning russet, I had a major task awaiting me.

Ever since arriving in the spring I had cut wood simply as we needed it—a few armfuls at a time. But now, with winter coming on, we faced a different situation. This was not the Agua Fria—this was Sierra County where a snowfall up to several feet in depth several times during the winter would be the rule rather than the exception. A winter's supply of wood was mandatory. The man who waits until it snows to gather wood is a fool.

I knew I could cut several cords of wood in a week, providing I devoted full time to the job. I also knew the sooner I got to it the better. So, turning the mining duties over to Dot, I sharpened ax and cross-cut saw and picked out a couple of oak trees which appeared to offer good woodcutting possibilities.

Dot mined on the river each day until midafternoon, then, because I was so busy cutting wood I was not even taking time off to hunt, she would catch a mess of trout to provide meat for our evening meal.

At end of the week I had more than three cords of good, solid oak wood stacked in the half of the storage shed not occupied by the Chevvy—and both Dot and I were damned sick of fish.

On the afternoon I finished stacking the last of the wood, Dot came home with another mess of trout. I nearly gagged when I looked at them.

"As a change of menu how would you like some fresh venison liver for dinner," I asked.

"I'll have bacon and onions ready to throw into the frying pan any time you arrive with the liver. I'm as tired of trout as you are," said Dot.

Dot put the trout in the cooler which I had rebuilt following the visit from the bear, and armed with the 30-30, I started out to collect the venison. A steep little side canyon led north from the cabin, and up this ravine I traveled. I worked slowly, quietly up the narrow draw, watching the opposite side. Any deer I spooked would likely cross the ravine and put himself within easy gun range as he climbed the other hillside.

It still was a week until the opening of deer season, but hunting seasons didn't mean much those days, and I had no intention of going another day without fresh meat.

I had progressed perhaps a half mile when I suddenly heard the thump of hoofs on the hillside below me. A spike buck dodged through the timber, and a moment later crossed the ravine and started up the other side.

The little buck crossed a small clearing, disappeared into a fringe of manzanita brush, and came out into a larger clearing about a hundred yards away.

Then, as deer so often do when they are only mildly frightened, the buck stopped, peering back over his shoulder to determine exactly what it was that had startled him.

At the sound of the shot he dropped, tumbling stone dead, heels over horns into the canyon. But, as the buck I had shot at fell, I detected from the corner of my eye, another movement on the hillside to my right.

I swung around in time to catch a single glimpse of the biggest buck deer I had ever seen, just as he was disappearing into the timber. He was huge. A giant. And although I had really only seen him for an instant, his image was indelibly impressed on my mind. Four huge points on each side of a rack of horns that seemed large enough to fit an elk.

Even had I been able, I would not have shot the big buck then. I was never a trophy hunter, and one buck at a time was enough. But as I stood there I made up my mind that should the big buck and I cross paths again when I needed meat, his horns would decorate our cabin wall. The chances of such a happening, however, I felt were slim. With deer season coming on I felt he would more than likely become the trophy of some other hunter. Anyway, I was too busy to waste time hunting for any individual buck simply because he carried a big rack of antlers.

Deer season arrived, and by the time it drew to a close in mid-October we already had experienced our first rains. We mined on the river each day we could, but storms in Sierra County are cold. We knew there would be many more days in the winter here we would be unable to work than there were on the Agua Fria.

During the latter weeks of October and into early November we enjoyed true autumn weather. Indian summer. Oak leaves were tinted with yellows and warm browns, and water maples suddenly became clumps of golden flame. Dogwood leaves turned their usual scarlet, and a score of other trees and plants added varied shades of color. The midday sun still was warm, but there was a hint of frost in the air in the mornings and after the sun went down.

Then, suddenly, the weather changed. Dark, brooding storm clouds moved in. It was cold, even during midmorning, and I expected rain by night.

Shortly before noon Dot stopped work at the sluice box to gather sticks of driftwood for a fire on which to heat the coffee-pot, but I stopped her.

"Honey, it's just too miserable to keep on working out here this afternoon. Let's go back to the cabin and call it a day. We can eat lunch there."

Dot was completely agreeable, for her hands were virtually blue with cold. She had been picking the larger rocks out of the sluice box as I shoveled gravel, and there is no colder work when the weather is miserable.

We finished lunch in the warm cabin, with the fire blazing pleasantly. I could have very well enjoyed a nap, but instead, with a storm threatening, I decided to replenish our supply of venison.

Winchester over my shoulder, I started up the trail into the same ravine where I had killed the spike buck some six weeks earlier.

For nearly an hour I climbed slowly, following the narrow, winding path beyond the spot where I had killed the little buck. Try as I might to move quietly, dried, fallen leaves rattled beneath my feet, too often warning game of my approach. Twice I heard deer jump and run, but neither time could I so much as catch a glimpse of them.

Then, gradually, the canyon widened, breaking into a series of pine- and oak-clad flats. Ideal deer country. There were pine needles on the ground now, making traveling considerably more quiet. I worked through the first little flat, across the second, and was just on the lip of a third small pine-covered plateau when I saw him. He stood stock-still, a huge, Roman-nosed old buck watching my every move. His broad antlers were half-hidden by the small cedar tree under which he was standing.

I stopped, tried to raise the rifle slowly in order not to startle him, but the instant he realized he was discovered the buck became a gray streak darting among the trees.

My first shot was somewhere behind him, and the second one threw up dust under his feet. A third bullet missed its mark. It was my last chance as I squeezed off the fourth shot. The rifle barked and suddenly, as though the earth had been jerked from beneath him, the big buck was down.

I ran the hundred yards to where the buck lay. He was not even kicking and I knew he was stone dead.

For several moments I admired the big deer. Sleek gray coat, white muzzle—an indication of age—his sweeping antlers with spread of at least thirty inches, and four perfect points on each side, made this buck a perfect trophy.

For a moment I felt a wave of remorse at having killed such a magnificent animal. I had never seen a bigger buck, and I was sure he was the same one I had seen six weeks earlier.

But now the work would start, for it was going to be a real job to get that huge carcass to the cabin. The best thing, I decided, would be to skin the buck where he lay, then pack the venison to the cabin in quarters. "Enough meat to last us half the winter," I told myself.

I pulled out my heavy jackknife, opened it, and at the same instant, grabbed the buck by the antlers. That simple act was like the releasing of a spring.

One instant my hand was gripping the deer's antlers, and the next I was flying through the air. The buck was on his feet and I was rolling downhill end over end into a tree.

For an instant the big deer stood watching me, stamping his big front feet. Hair on the back of his neck bristled, his eyes were green with fury. I knew he was going to attack, and painfully I struggled to my feet and took a stout grip on my knife. The rifle, leaning against a tree, was too far away to do me any good.

The buck advanced a couple steps, then another, head low, antlers menacing. I saw the bullet wound which had knocked him down—a narrow grazed mark across his forehead which had scarcely drawn blood. The impact of the bullet had rendered him only momentarily unconscious.

Just as I was preparing for his lunge, the buck whirled and was gone. I stood there bewildered, still gripping the knife, wondering at the miracle which had turned the big deer's attack to flight.

Then I saw her. Ladybug—all fifteen pounds of her—came racing up the trail full tilt to leap into my lap, lick my face, and yip happily at having found me. She had been following my track, and upon hearing the shots had come running to get in on the excitement.

It was the arrival of the little dog that frightened off the buck, and, I am certain that had she not arrived and that big deer had carried out his attack, he would have killed me. I never saw the buck again, and to be truthful, I was damned glad of it.

December, and winter storms began in earnest. Rain and snow often halted our mining, and even on clear days bitter cold and high water made work difficult. It was even hard to build a fire along the river to cook lunch or get warm. Rain and constant moisture had saturated every kind of fuel. Dot's efforts to light a fire with wet wood usually resulted in expenditure of the larger part of a box of wooden matches, considerable smoke, some sulphurous language, but little heat.

Old Dan, a retired Downieville miner and prospector, had told me of a small hydraulic mining claim he owned, only a couple of miles from town. "You ain't gonna get rich on it," Dan warned, "but I think a man could make eating money there for a while."

The thing that interested me was that it was on a sunny slope, and it would be a nice place to work in the winter. During the last of the hydraulic mining operations, said Dan, a pretty fair-sized rock slide had come down into the pit and covered part of its bedrock floor.

The miners had washed away all but the biggest boulders, some larger than automobiles. The pay was such they did not bother moving the big rocks. "There's money under those boulders if you can break them or move them," said Dan. "One reason they've never been moved is because it's only at this time of year enough water accumulates in that little gully at the edge of the pit to run a rocker or even a gold pan. You're welcome to mine it if you want."

The pit was only four or five miles from our cabin and we could drive to within less than a hundred yards of it in the Chevvy. Anything, we agreed, would be better than the damp cold of the river, so we loaded in the necessary tools and started for Dan's claim.

The hydraulic pit was perhaps two-hundred yards long, seventy-five yards wide, and the embankment on the uphill side of it was about seventy-five feet high. At one edge of the pit the bedrock was strewn with large boulders and considerable rubble. Under these was supposed to be the gold. I picked out a couple of big slabs of rock on the edge of the boulder field, which looked breakable, and attacked them with the sledgehammer. Afterward, we cleaned up the bedrock under them and panned it.

I will say this for old Dan. He didn't exaggerate when he predicted we would not get rich. A day's damned hard work netted us $1.35, but we could eat on it, and it was away from the gloomy river. Furthermore, there was lots of dead manzanita brush around the pit that made wonderful wood on cold days, if we decided on a fire.

But breaking rocks with a sledgehammer is slow, hard work. I figured if I could dynamite the boulders I could work a much greater area in a day. By working a larger area, I should be able to make enough to pay for the blasting powder and make a bigger profit, too, I told Dot. Into Downieville we went, and came back from town with a fifty-pound box of dynamite, blasting caps, and fuse. The entire bill came to about fifteen dollars.

Two or three sticks of dynamite would crack a boulder enough that I could throw the broken pieces out of the way. I'll say this for the blasting. It was a helluva lot easier than swinging a sledge.

However, as for profit, after deducting cost of the dynamite, and the gasoline we used driving back and forth from our cabin, we averaged about a dollar and a half per day.

It was interesting work. Everyone around the country must have thought we had a really big mining operation going, for about twice-a-day the thunder of our dynamite blasts would go echoing up and down the canyon. Certainly it was better than the cold, wet canyon in winter, and we often had visitors at our diggings.

Old Dan came rattling out from town in his battered pickup truck at least twice a week. Now and then Tony came to visit us, and once Judge Robbins stopped by to "find out what the hell all this noise and blasting is all about."

Dan would perch himself on a big boulder where we would be scraping bedrock, fire up his evil-smelling, short-stemmed pipe and spin his tales of the early mining days. Dan had been a teamster before he turned to mining. As a young man, he also had ridden "shotgun" on the horse-drawn mail stages from Downieville, Alleghany, and other Sierra County towns to Nevada City and Grass Valley. Dan quit the stage guard job, he said, one day after he observed a man in the underbrush heading for the stage. He was just tightening up on the triggers of a buckshot-filled sawed-off shotgun when the man stepped into the road. It was his best friend who had been out fishing and wanted a ride back to town.

Now, in his eighties, Dan was suffering increasingly from rheumatism, living simply on meager savings and a small pension. We wanted the old man to accept at least 25 percent of the money we took from his claim. He shoved it aside—would have no part of it. "When you find a nugget the size of your fist, then I'll take half of it," he'd say.

But Dan had another mining claim, one higher up in the mountains, a gravel channel operation he claimed was rich.

"Now that's the place I want you kids to work," he would say. "I've made good money there—I could make good money there now if I wasn't such a danged old crip. Next summer I want you to take a look at it, I know you'll want to work it. That's the place where I'll go shares with you."

Freezing weather arrived, but except for times when snow or rain was actually falling, we continued to work each day. First chore of the morning would be to gather loads of dried, scrub manzanita that covered the hillside above the mine pit, and get a good, roaring fire going. Few types of wood burn hotter than manzanita. Then, on hands and knees, we would clean the bedrock and wash the scrapings through the little sluice box I had set up in the ravine at the edge of the pit. We stopped often to warm our half-frozen fingers and creaking joints at the fire.

On rainy days or when there actually was snow on the ground we pretty much stuck to the cabin, and more often than not we would have visitors.

Dan would come by, and quite often Tony Lavazolla or others from Downieville stopped in and usually ended by staying the afternoon. And the talk always turned to gold and mining.

Sierra County, since early gold rush days, produced nearly $150,000,000 in gold. The old Tin Cup diggings, a 60 x 60-foot claim, produced $80,000 in the space of a few weeks. The claim got its name from the fact that three men filled a tin cup with nuggets every day they operated the diggings.

History of the famous mines and mining camps such as Forest and Brandy City, Alleghany, Goodyear Bar, all were familiar to Dan and Tony. They spent long afternoons spinning yarns about such mines as the Brown Bear, New York, Kirkpatrick, the Golden Hub, and City of Six. Each produced up to half-a-million dollars in raw gold.

Famous hardrock mines that produced millions included the Kate Hardy, the Oriental, and the Sixteen-to-One, which was operating in the Alleghany district while we lived in Sierra County. The Sixteen-to-One actually ran profitably until 1965, long after Dot and I left Sierra County and quit mining for a living. The mine, fabulously rich in raw gold, was closed, according to its owner, not because of shortage of gold but because operating expenses—labor and material—became too high. The price of gold remained the same at thirty-five dollars an ounce, while miners' wages doubled, tripled, then quadrupled and climbed still higher.

"I don't think there's ever been a gold mine that produced any appreciable amount of gold in which there wasn't at least some high-grading," remarked Tony one afternoon. (High-grading is theft of gold by miners employed in a mine.)

"There was this miner—worked at several of the hardrock mines in and around Grass Valley and Nevada City—came up here and went to work at the Sixteen-to-One. Pretty nice fellow, he seemed. Rented a cabin in Alleghany in which he and his wife lived. He stopped in at the hotel once in a while to talk. One day he mentioned he had filed a mining claim on the river a few miles down from here. From the way he talked, it may not have been too far from this cabin.

"Anyway, I didn't see this fella for some time. One afternoon he walks in and said he understood that sometimes I bought gold. I told him I sometimes bought specimen gold, but not the fine, river gold like he would be getting at his claim. This guy didn't say a word. He just pulled a tobacco can out of his pocket and poured a half-dozen ounces of the prettiest quartz gold I've ever seen, right out there on the table.

"'Oh, I got lucky and hit a little quartz ledge that's putting out some pretty good gold,' he tells me.

"I looked at this guy. What kind of a damned fool do you think I am? You're working at the Sixteen-to-One and you file a placer claim on the river where you can make a dollar or so a day in fine gold if you're lucky. Then you come in here with this good-looking quartz gold and tell me you got it out of a quartz ledge on the river.

"Now you get the hell outa here, I told him, before I take both you and this gold to the superintendent of the Sixteen-to-One. I don't particularly like any thief, but I especially don't like a thief who thinks I'm damned fool enough to believe a yarn like you've just told me!

"I never saw this guy again," said Tony, "but I heard later he quit the Sixteen-to-One a short time later. A few days after he quit he bought a brand-new car in Grass Valley."

There were other stories on those winter days, one in particular which Dan told, that have intrigued me ever since.

As all men will do, Dan may have elaborated his stories a bit, or dramatized them, but Dan never told an outright lie.

Dan was about eighty-two when he told the story, and he said the incident occurred when he was about twelve, which would have placed date of the happening around 1868.

Dan's father was a blacksmith in Sierra City, and a man of some financial means who was well respected in the community, Dan said. His father did no mining, but he was interested in gold, and on occasion, grubstaked prospectors whom he knew and trusted.

One summer night, said Dan, long after the family had gone to bed they were awakened by the barking of their dog and someone pounding on their front door. Armed with a shotgun, Dan's father answered the door, to find a prospector friend, whom he had grubstaked some weeks earlier, awaiting him.

Despite the fact it was after midnight, the prospector came in. Dan said he still can remember peeking down the stairs at his father and the prospector as they huddled around the kitchen table, inspecting white quartz rocks the prospector took from a saddlebag.

"Both the man and my dad were excited," said Dan. "I can remember my father swearing, which he did only when he was greatly agitated. The prospector stayed at our house all night, and next morning I heard the major part of the story."

It seems, according to Dan, the prospector was searching for gold-bearing gravel rather than a quartz ledge or seam, and spent most of his time exploring streams, ravines, and canyons. Then, with supplies running low, this fellow, who was somewhere north of the Sierra City and Downieville area started cross-country for Sierra City.

While following a deer trail with his pack horse, the prospector found his way blocked by a recently fallen pine tree.

The tree, for some reason, had uprooted and toppled over. Easiest way to get around it was to lead his horse around the uprooted tree stump, he said, and then he saw the exposed quartz rock. In uprooting, the tree had uncovered a quartz ledge several inches wide. Chunks of quartz still clung to the uprooted section, and more was exposed in the bottom of the hole created by the falling tree. The rock was literally laced with gold.

The prospector, keeping only his rifle, blankets, and some dried meat, dumped all of his other camping equipment out of his saddlebags and filled them with the rich gold ore. Carefully as possible, he buried his abandoned equipment and all evidence of the quartz rock in the stump hole. When finished, he said, not a bit of evidence of gold or quartz was visible. Even though it was then late in the day, the prospector headed for Sierra City and traveled more than twenty-four hours without sleep to reach Dan's father's home.

Next day, Dan's father and the prospector began organizing an expedition to reach the new gold strike. But secretive as they attempted to be, apparently talk of the strike, or at least suspicion of a strike, began to circulate. The prospector left Sierra City late in the afternoon to ride to Downieville for a couple of horses he had pastured near there. Although he was to return next morning he did not appear. Late that day the stage arrived, leading the prospector's horse which had been found wandering loose on the road. A search was organized and the body of the missing man was found about five miles from Downieville. He had been shot through the head.

But if the man who bushwhacked him thought the prospector carried a map, Dan is sure he was disappointed.

"I'm sure there was never a map drawn—there was no reason for one to be," said Dan. "That man—I can't remember his name, I was too young, and it was too long ago—knew that country so well he didn't need a map. He would not have drawn one for my father because he was going to take my father there."

Dan said his father scoured the country for years, whenever he could find the time, looking for evidence of the buried gold strike. At times, said Dan, he went with his father.

"It probably was pretty damned will hidden to begin with," said Dan, "and then to make matters worse, a couple years later a big forest fire swept through the country where we thought the mine was. The fire could have burned the remains of the fallen tree and left almost nothing to use as a landmark."

Dan closed his yarn by saying his father turned the quartz rock over to an assayer. The whole load weighed about a hundred pounds. When it was crushed and panned, the recovered gold was valued at more than two hundred dollars, which would have made that ore worth more than four thousand dollars a ton at the old price of gold. It would be worth eight thousand dollars a ton at present gold prices.

By April the weather had improved immeasurably and trees were well budded out. Spring was on its way, and the snow was melting in the high country. Dan kept talking about his other mining claim which he wanted us to work for him. We were pretty well finished cleaning up the hydraulic pit and were only waiting now for the snow to finish melting so we could tackle Dan's rich claim in the mountains.

As the weather improved, more snipers began showing up along the river again, and the first of the vacationers made their appearance.

The cattlemen who turn their livestock loose to graze in the mountains also arrived with herds of bawling white-faced cattle whose bells clanged and tunk-a-tunked on the hillsides and sometimes close outside our cabin windows, keeping us awake at night.

A vacationing couple and their three children arrived one evening and pitched their tent on a little flat not a hundred yards from our cabin. The flat also was inhabited by a half-dozen lazy old cows who looked upon it as their special bedding ground.

The camper and his family shooed the cows from the flat, pitched their tent, and by dark had a very respectable-looking camp established. I don't know exactly what time they went to bed, but when we next awakened, their campfire had burned down to just a bed of glowing coals.

Sometime after midnight Dot and I were awakened by screams, curses, frightened cries of children, and the clanging of cowbells.

Cows are curious. Some time after activity around the vacationers' camp had died down, the old cows decided to pay it a visit. Apparently the man or his wife awakened to hear a cow stomping around the tent and yelled to scare her away. There was not one cow, there were several cows. They were frightened and ran.

Only problem was, that as they ran, at least one cow's feet tangled in the tent ropes. As she fled, she took the tent with her.

Trapped under the fallen canvas, the family amid shouts, curses, and cries of fright, extricated themselves from beneath it on one side while the cow untangled herself on the other side.

Adding to the difficulties, the cow had managed to drag one end of the tent across the nearby campfire before getting loose, and it now broke into merry flame.

Goaded by Dot, I climbed into pants and shoes and went

down to help extinguish the tent fire. By the time the fire was out, the tent had a hole burned in it just large enough for a cow to run through.

We served the somewhat shaken campers coffee and hot chocolate at the cabin. They spent the remainder of the night bunked on the cabin porch, safely out of reach of cows.

CHAPTER XIV

JACKPOT

WORK IN THE HYDRAULIC PIT DIGGINGS WAS FINISHED, AND FOR nearly a month we had been sniping back on the river. Spring was slipping into early summer when one evening Ladybug's barking announced the arrival of a visitor. In the distance I could hear the familiar rattle of old Dan's dilapidated pickup truck as it made its way slowly down the hill.

Dan drove an automobile about the same way he used to drive a horse, allowing it to sort of pick its own way among the ruts and chuckholes, setting its own pace. The truck pulled into the yard and stopped. Dan dismounted, stretched his creaking joints, and came ambling over to the porch where Dot and I were waiting. The old man knew us too well to bother with such formalities as shaking hands, even though he had not seen us for nearly a month. Instead, he greeted us casually, accepted the chair I offered, and after making himself comfortable, paused to light his pipe.

Dan leaned back in his chair, took a deep drag from the smelly, blackened old pipe, and exhaled slowly.

"Well, I reckon I'm goin' to head up into the high country to the mine about day after tomorrow. Thought you kids might want to go up with me and get started.

"I run into one of the Forest Service boys the other day and he had been part of the way in. Sez the snow's pretty well off the road now, and except for a few fallen trees he could have driven all the way to the mine."

It was the news Dot and I had been waiting for since early spring. If this mine was half as good as Dan said it was, both of us felt we could make more in a week there than we could in a month sniping for fine gold on the river.

We sat for a long time on the porch that balmy spring evening talking over plans for the trip and for our mining operation.

There were two cabins there—shacks, Dan called them. One was really an old toolshed and blacksmith shop, but it had a stove and a bunk in it, said Dan. The other one was a larger one-room log cabin which had been built some forty years earlier.

"They ain't a whole lot to look at, but they'll keep the rain off our heads—at least some of the rain," commented Dan. "At least they'll sure as hell be better than trying to camp outdoors. It'll still be colder than Billy-be-damned up there now. The elevation of that mine is just a little better than seven thousand feet."

The mine itself was a small, underground gravel channel, Dan said. In places, the channel was virtually barren and carried no gold value, but then suddenly there would be a rich spot, and a single car of ore could be worth a hundred dollars or more.

The mine was located in what is known as a "lava cap" country, an area of volcanic geology which at one time was covered by a flow of basaltic lava. The gravel deposit we would be mining was nothing more than an ancient stream bed that a few million years ago had been covered by the lava flow.

We discussed with Dan the mining method we would use, and what we would take with us in the way of food and equipment.

There was no mill at the mine. The gold-bearing gravel simply was brought out of the mine in an ore car and dumped into big sluice boxes. The gravel ran through a series of sluice boxes for nearly a hundred feet, then the tailings from the boxes washed into a steep, deep-sided little ravine below the mine.

"At times we've had a little trouble saving the gold," said Dan. "Some of that gravel is pretty badly cemented and doesn't break up too good as it goes through the sluice boxes. I know we've lost gold at times—but we've always managed to save some too. It may not be a big enough operation for a company, but it's a good little mine for a couple of people who know what they're doing and aren't afraid of work."

It was nearly midnight before we finally said goodbye to Dan. He stood up, stretched, knocked the ashes from his pipe, and started slowly for his pickup. It was then he dropped the bomb. Although at the time it did not even seem to be a firecracker.

"One thing—we gotta kinda be careful of rattlesnakes up there. Seems awful high elevation for rattlesnakes, but they're there. Kinda think there's a den of 'em up there in the rimrocks back of the mine somewhere, because every year, just after the time the snow goes off, we see quite a few of them. They kinda distract a man when they get too thick."

Shortly after sunup, two mornings later, Dot and I threw the last of our camping gear into the Chevvy and with Dan's old pickup leading the way, started for the mountain gold mine.

In airline miles Dan's mine was probably not more than eight or ten miles from our cabin. By road, the route we had to travel, the distance was between sixteen and twenty miles. And a winding, twisting, narrow road it was. It had been an old wagon road at one time, and since the last wagon traveled it there had been damned few improvements. We turned off the highway and started up the mountain side. Before we had gone a hundred yards I had the Chevvy down in low gear, and for the next three hours I don't think I ever got up more speed than five miles per hour.

The farther up the mountain we traveled the steeper and rougher the road became. The road was exactly the same width as the car and not an inch wider. Gripping Ladybug with her left hand, Dot clung for dear life to the door of the car with her right. She was saying nothing, but out of the corner of my eye I could see she was not exactly enjoying the trip.

The first few miles led through groves of black oak and Ponderosa pine, but as we climbed higher we ran into a belt of Douglas fir, then white fir, and the air began to feel considerably cooler. We stopped twice during the first hour to cut small trees out of the road. Then, as we rounded a bend, I came upon Dan and his pickup stopped in front of a huge downed fir which blocked our passage.

The tree was nearly three feet in diameter and lay squarely across the road. There was no way to get around it, and I had visions of being forced to return to camp. But I had underestimated Dan, both in resourcefulness and strength.

As I stood there surveying the scene Dan walked around to the back of his pickup and pulled out a six-foot, two-man crosscut saw. "Come on, Java, we'll just have to take a piece out of the middle of this toothpick," he said. Not only did he have the saw, he had sledgehammer, steel wedges, and a crowbar. Dan had made this trip too many other years not to be fully prepared.

And it was with surprising strength the old man attacked that big log. With one of us on each end of the saw, we had the log cut through in less than a half hour. In little more than an hour we were on our way up the hill again.

And now the country changed again.

The heavy stands of timber thinned until there were only scattered groves of red fir and weather twisted tamaracks. The country also had begun to level off. We were nearing the top now, and it began to take on a barren, volcanic look. There was a creek below us, steep-sided and rough, lined with stunted mountain willow and quaking aspen.

"Look," Dot cried, "I can see a cabin—that must be the mine!" Upcanyon, ahead of us a half mile, I also could make out the shape of what appeared to be a building on the edge of a small mountain meadow. The little canyon we were following seemed to head at the meadow and its stream originated there.

Five minutes later we pulled up and stopped beside Dan's pickup which was parked in front of a gray, weather-beaten log cabin. Windows of the cabin were boarded up, and snow had broken down one corner of the roof.

A sharp alpine wind made me shiver as I climbed from the Chevvy, and I saw there still was a little drift of snow in the shade behind the cabin. A second building constructed of sawed lumber—presumably this was the blacksmith shop and toolshed—stood some fifty yards away.

"Well, here she is, what there is of her," said Dan. "The mine's right up around the corner of the hill there. Over there," he said, waving at where water running from the meadow began to form the creek, "is where we sluice the gravel. You can't see 'em from here because of the grass, but there's rails all the way across there to run the ore car to the sluice boxes."

I was all for looking over the mine and mining possibilities right now, but Dot would have none of it.

"Before we do anything else, let's get that cabin opened up and get moved into it," demanded Dot. "We've got from now on for mining, but I'm not going to find myself setting up camp and cooking dinner over a campfire after dark."

The cabin was not exactly the latest word in housing. You could see blue sky through one corner of the roof where snow had popped a rafter and its weight had smashed through the shingles. The chinking between the logs that formed the walls was pretty well gone, and we could get a fair view of the countryside through any wall we looked at. Mice had built nests on shelves, and a packrat had a fairly respectable-sized home of sticks and trash in one corner.

We cleaned the place out with a shovel, then Dot swept the floor with a fir bough broom. In one end of the single large room stood a huge cast-iron stove. I gathered armloads of wood, built a fire in it, and within minutes the sides of the old stove were glowing red. The stove radiated heat in all directions and in a much shorter time than we thought possible, despite a gaping roof and cracks in the walls, the interior of the old cabin was comfortably warm.

There was a rap on the door and old Dan, who had been giving his living quarters in the blacksmith shop their annual renovation, was standing there.

"If you're ready, let's take a walk over to the tunnel, I'm anxious to see it myself and see how it fared through the winter."

It was only a quarter mile from cabin to mine tunnel, but at 7500-feet elevation a walk of even that distance makes a person breathe hard.

We rounded the little point that allowed us to view the mine entrance, and suddenly old Dan stopped dead in his tracks.

Where the mouth of the mine tunnel should have been there was only a pile of boulders and rubble. The entire portal area had caved. Hundreds of tons of rock and earth had come cascading down, and the entire front of the tunnel was gone, flattened. The tunnel was filled for many yards back into the hill.

For several minutes the old man did not even speak.

"Would you look at that—I'll be double damned—just look at that!" Old Dan stood there slowly cursing, not so much in anger but in the same tone he would have used had he been praying. He was astonished—thunderstruck—by what he saw.

We stood there, the three of us, looking in complete dismay at what had been Dan's mine. I knew that to try and reopen it would be a task bigger than I would want to tackle. Here was a full summer's work just in opening up the mouth of the mine.

"Well, it's been a nice trip up here and we've seen some pretty country. It's too late to try to go back to the river tonight, so let's go back to the cabin and eat supper."

Dot looked at me with a wry grin. "I'm not too disappointed," she said. "I knew it was too good to be true, and anyway, I like it down there on the river real well."

But despite what Dot or I, or what old Dan said, it was a badly disappointed group of three who sat down to dinner in the old cabin that night. We finished eating, and I rolled a cigarette for Dot and myself while Dan stoked up his pipe.

"Now I know you kids are disappointed," Dan said. "For that matter, so am I. But before we leave in the morning, there's something I want you to try. You know, I told you we sometimes lost gold because of the cemented gravel—well, there were times when we lost a hell of a lot. Gravel just washed through the sluice boxes in big gobs and didn't break up. All held together with rusted iron pyrites and manganese. Now it's had time to soften and air slack. It might just be worthwhile to take a look at those tailings that have been poured down that little creek for the last half-dozen years.

"This old mine," Dan went on, "is about as old as I am. I never got my hands on it until about twenty years ago. They tell me in the early days the Chinamen used to pay the fellows who ran this mine to let them work the creek where he dumped his tailings. Ain't no Chinamen left round here no more, but they wasn't nobody's damn fools either. If they thought it was worth buying the mining rights to those tailings each year they must have done pretty well.

"Before we leave tomorrow morning I'd like you to take a look at those tailings—pan a few of them at least. They might surprise you."

I tried to appear interested in order not to hurt the old man's feelings, but truthfully I had few intentions of wasting any time next morning panning or sampling any of the old mine tailings in that creek. We sat around the stove for a while, but shortly after dark old Dan excused himself and shuffled off to the blacksmith shop where he had spread his bed. A short time later Dot and I also crawled into the blankets. It had been a long and disappointing day.

I awoke at daylight, and even though it was early June there was a skim of frost on the ground outside. We had slept none too warm, even under our heavy blankets. I jumped out of bed and hurriedly stoked up a fire in the big stove.

By the time I had it roaring Dot was up and dressed and the coffeepot was bubbling. Dan, his coat collar pulled up around his ears, came hobbling up from his shack, glad to bask his rheumatism in the warmth of the stove while Dot fried bacon and eggs. The sun was barely hitting the tops of the lava-capped ridges and rimrocks above us when we sat down to breakfast.

I intended to get an early start down the hill, for I figured if I hurried I still could get in an afternoon's mining on the river. While Dot washed the dishes I loaded blankets and our meager camping gear into the Chevvy.

It was then we discovered the flat tire on Dan's pickup. The left front tire was completely flat, and to make matters worse, Dan had no spare. It was a matter of pull off the flat tire, patch the tube, put the tire back together again, and pump it up by hand. The only redeeming feature was that both Dan and I had tire pumps and tire-patching materials. They were standard equipment in every car in those days, and a flat tire was looked upon simply as a slight delaying inconvenience rather than a tragedy.

I suppose it took a half hour, certainly not more than forty-five minutes to patch and put the tire back on Dan's truck. During that time I had paid scant attention to Dot or what she was doing. I tightened the last lug nut on the wheel, stood up to brush the dirt from my hands and looked around for my wife: she was nowhere to be seen.

I called out to her, but there was no answer. I shouted again. No reply. Puzzled more than worried, I looked around again, just in time to see Dot scrambling up over the lip of the steep creekbank from the spot where the mine tailings had piled up.

In one hand Dot was holding a gold pan, and with her other arm she was waving at us. She also was shouting something, but the noise of the nearby creek garbled her words.

Dan and I started toward Dot, who was hurrying as fast as she could, nearly spilling the pan she was holding. She was completely breathless when we met in the middle of the meadow. Gasping for breath, my excited wife shoved the gold pan toward us. There were beads of sweat on her face and her hair was in disarray. But the gold pan she thrust at us, still wet from the creek where she had been panning, contained a dozen glistening little nuggets each the size of a large grain of rice.

Exactly what I said I'm not sure, but the people in Downieville, twenty miles away, probably heard me holler.

Old Dan was virtually jumping up and down, pounding me on the back with one hand and hammering on Dot with the other. He hit Dot so hard I was afraid he was going to make her spill the gold pan. "I knew it was here—I knew it was here, by gads! It just hadda be here!" shouted the old man.

I ran for the Chevvy, grabbed sluice box and shovel and headed for the creek. By noon I had sluiced deep into the lower deposit of tailings. We cleaned up the sluice box to see how we had been doing and I estimated we had about twenty-five dollars.

Dot was still so excited she did not even want to stop for lunch, but finally we took time out to eat hastily thrown together sandwiches then rushed back to work.

The gravel itself ranged in size from pebbles to round, washed stone about the size of my fist. Unlike the gravel we had been working on the river, this was stained brown, and orange and black from the iron pyrites and manganese which was heavily distributed through it. It was easy to see what had happened over the years.

Much of the cemented gravel, held tightly together by a clayish type of deposit, plus the encrustations of rotted iron pyrites, had not broken up when it was originally washed through the sluice boxes. Now it had lain in the open air and water and the material which originally had bound it together had broken down. The gravel crumbled and washed clean now as it passed through our sluice box, leaving the gold it carried with it in our sluice box riffles.

Why old Dan and his various partners, since they had run the mine, had not sampled those tailings I will never know. Certainly Dan was a good enough miner to realize what was happening, and certainly, the former mine owners and the Chinese miners had known the tailings carried value.

I think it was simply this: Dan and his partners had made money in this mine. Enough money that while they certainly did not get rich, they did not worry much about the percentage they lost.

Actually, the gravel they normally took from the mine was not as rich as what we were finding in these tailings. We actually were mining the concentrated gravel, the best of what had been lost over a period of perhaps ten years. We worked until the sun tipped over the western ridgetops above us. Then, far more exhausted than we realized, we trudged back to the cabin.

We had no gold scales with us, but as Dot cooked supper I carefully washed and cleaned up our day's take in the gold pan. Dan and I looked over the little heap of rough pieces in the pan and estimated conservatively that we had a hundred and twenty-five dollars. This was not the bright, shiny gold such as we found in the river. The iron and manganese had stained it until it was almost black. Only here and there did it have the yellow sheen of gold.

We had no nitric acid with us to remove the discoloration from the gold, but I remembered a trick the Chinese miners had used to clean gold when I was a kid. I dumped the day's take into a little buckskin pouch and began slapping the pouch lightly against a flat rock. By the time supper was ready the gold had polished until it was as bright as if I had used acid on it.

In places the gravel was several feet deep, held back by large boulders which had formed more or less of a dam in the bottom of the ravine. I pried and broke the boulders to get them out of the way, for there was little room to work in the bottom of the narrow ravine. The gravel was backed up for a distance of about two hundred feet. In some places it was four feet deep, in others it had a depth of only inches. I estimated it would require about two weeks to work the entire deposit.

For a week we worked from daylight to dark, and not once did we net less than a hundred dollars at end of a day's labor. We ran low on food and while Dot and I worked, Dan drove to town to bring in fresh supplies. We were so engrossed we even forgot what day of the week it was, and worked right through Sunday.

Each day it was becoming warmer, and the snow around the cabin and on the shaded slopes had disappeared.

It was while eating lunch on our tenth day at the mine that Dot suddenly glanced out the door and let out a shriek which almost shook the shingles loose . . . "Snake—rattlesnake!" And, sure enough, slithering across the yard not six feet in front of the cabin door was a big, diamondback timber rattler. He was fully three feet long.

I grabbed the .410 shotgun and with a single shot took care of the snake situation. The charge of shot, fired at close range, virtually disintegrated the snake's flat, ugly head. We finished lunch and while I took time out to chop some wood, Dot took the water bucket and started for the spring. The spring was about fifty yards from the cabin, and just as she reached it, I heard my wife let out another shriek. I knew without even asking what it was.

There, coiled beside the trail, was another adult rattler, his head was drawn back and he was angrily sounding that vicious, warning rattle. I didn't bother to run for the shotgun, I simply killed the snake with the ax.

Dot already had filled her bucket at the spring when she saw the snake. She had yelled and run still carrying the bucket. Despite her fright, she had arrived at the cabin without spilling a drop of water.

Dan, who had been taking it all in and saying little until now, suddenly enlightened us.

Methodically, he tamped a load of tobacco into his pipe, carefully lit it, and took a couple of deep drags before he spoke.

"Remember, couple weeks ago afore we started up here I told ya we kinda had to watch for these buzztails. Well, this happens every year 'bout this time. Must be a big den of the damned things up there in the rimrock underneath the lava cap someplace. First warm days, out they come. For a while they get pretty thick around here—kinda have to watch your step. Course, they scatter out pretty soon, and by midsummer sometimes you go a day or two without seeing a snake."

I looked at Dot and she wore about the same expression as if old Dan had told her he had just lighted the fuse to a box of dynamite we were sitting on.

"Ain't never had nobody get bit by one of them though we had a few pretty close calls," said Dan, as if that were any real consolation to my wife.

"I really don't care how rich this place is, or how much gold we're getting—I'm all for getting out of here, now," Dot asserted. "I'd rather be poor and healthy than rich and snakebit."

It took me a full hour to talk Dot into staying at least a few more days. The first thing I had to do was get old Dan out of the cabin and turned off of his rattlesnake stories. Just about the time I'd get Dot talked into staying, Dan would come up with another one of his yarns about somebody finding a snake coiled up on the foot of his bed or some other damned fool thing. Then Dot would immediately grab things and begin packing again.

We decided to stay on, snakes or no snakes. We tied Ladybug in the cabin where we hoped she would encounter no rattlers and went back to work. By now it was midafternoon. We saw no more snakes for nearly an hour, and then Dan, on his way back to the cabin to get a crowbar for me, killed two snakes right in front of the blacksmith shop. Of course, he had to tell Dot about them.

We finished mining for the day, working until almost dark, and the gold we got was even heavier than usual. I estimated we had well over a hundred dollars.

Morning came, and we were back to work at sunup, and the snakes were still with us.

We had been working less than an hour when a big rattler came crawling down the steep side of the ravine. He was only about fifteen feet from us when I spotted him and dispatched him with a shovel. It was a big, thick snake, light colored from having been in hibernation and it had twelve segments to its rattles.

By ten o'clock I had killed two more snakes, one that Dot spotted and one that I saw coming down the bank toward the creek.

We stopped for lunch, and on the way to the cabin I killed yet another rattler. By now, Dot and I were both so jumpy that if someone had sneezed we would have lost a year's growth. All we could see and all we could think of was rattlesnakes.

Lunch, at least, was uneventful. We returned to the ravine and I leaned over to pick up my shovel which was lying beside the sluice box. Suddenly, I let out a yell and made a standing broadjump that under other circumstances would have set an Olympic record. There, coiled and buzzing loudly, was another big rattlesnake lying alongside my shovel handle. My bare hand, when I reached for the shovel, had been within three inches of that snake's fangs.

"Come on," I said. "We're getting the hell outa here now. This gold can wait. I want to be able to enjoy what we already have. Let's start packing."

Dot was in complete agreement, and even old Dan put up no argument. He had almost stepped on a rattler that morning which he had not told us about. Furthermore, he admitted, this was not the first time he had been run out of here by rattlesnakes.

"It'll be waiting for us here in September and the snakes will all have gone to bed," said Dan. "We'll finish cleaning 'er up then and the gold will be just as good."

I fully agreed, and little more than an hour later with our supplies loaded and the cabin and blacksmith shop boarded up again, we started down the hill.

Just as we were leaving the flat where the mine was located I stopped and as a parting gesture killed one more rattlesnake that was lying in the road.

Old Dan, following us in his pickup, leaned out the window and hollered: "No use bothering with the damned things now, Java. You kill one of 'em and two more come to his funeral."

It was dark when we arrived at our cabin on the river, and an hour later, while Dot fried bacon and eggs, Dan and I weighed our profits. We had exactly forty ounces, amounting to just a shade under $1400—a pretty good haul for eleven days' work.

We tried to split the money even with Dan but he would have no part of it. Finally, after an hour's argument, he agreed to accept a third, then complained because he said he was cheating us.

Old Dan has been gone for a lot of years, but we still talk of him and miss him. There were damned few finer men than old Dan.

CHAPTER XV

THE BEST YEARS OF OUR LIVES

IT SEEMS AN ACCEPTED FACT IN THE PUBLIC MIND, AND EVEN among other miners, that the fellow who brings in a bit of gold now and then is just a lucky stiff who happened to strike it rich.

"Old Joe sure was lucky to hit that pocket and take out all that money . . . Sure wish I had his rabbit's foot," they will say. Nothing is ever mentioned about the years it took "old Joe" to learn the skills of gold mining or of the weeks and months of hard work spent in taking out that gold.

Men came from the city during the days of the Depression to try and make a living panning for gold—men who never before had seen gold or a gold pan—and the only surprising thing is that they did not actually starve.

Saturday was usually our day in town, and our first stop was always the general store where we cashed our week's earnings of gold and replenished supplies.

I usually tried to attract as little attention as possible as I handed our little bottle of gold to be weighed out and exchanged for currency. But, more often than not, customers and hangers-on, and sometimes a tourist or two, crowded around the counter when they saw the store owner begin to set up his gold scales.

After completing transactions at the store we usually stopped in to talk to Judge Robbins or Tony. It was on one such visit, after returning from the rattlesnake mine, that Judge Robbins asked a favor of me.

The judge and I were seated in his barber shop talking mining and catching up on the news of the past week when a tall, blond youth clad in faded, patched overalls and tattered shirt strode past the shop.

"There," said the judge, pointing toward the young man, "goes the unluckiest human being I know. He's a good kid, came here about a year ago—says he's an orphan—and took up mining. How he's managed to exist I really don't know. He doesn't know the first thing about mining, but he works from daylight to dark. Lives in an old tent up the river a couple of miles—and I think there are times he actually goes hungry.

"I've helped him out a couple of times, but he won't accept a loan—real independent he is," said the judge.

"First thing you know, winter will be here again, and I just don't see how that kid is going to make it.

"You know, Jess, I like that kid—he's got a lot of guts—and I'd kind of look upon it as a personal favor if you and Dot would figure out a way to maybe give him a bit of a hand, let him work with you a while and at least teach him something about sniping for gold."

The boy—his nickname was "Happy"—was headed back toward his camp, and when Dot arrived at the barber shop a short time later, we talked over the judge's proposal with her.

"Poor kid, of course we can give him a hand," Dot told the judge. Then, turning to me, she said, "Jess, why don't you ride out to his camp and ask him if he'd work with you—tell him you need someone to help you move some heavy boulders. Tell him he can stay with us."

Happy was not unknown to me. I had seen him around town from time to time, and a couple of times I had seen him sniping on the river. I knew where his camp was located, but he had not even reached his camp when I caught up with him.

Trying to keep to the truth as much as possible, I told Happy that I was looking for someone to help me work a piece of ground down the river near our cabin, and that Judge Robbins had suggested him. The boy, I suppose he was about nineteen or twenty, gave me that grin which had earned him his nickname.

"Sure, I'll be glad to give you a hand, Mr. Coffey. I'm not doing much good where I'm working anyway, and it won't hurt for me to be away from my camp for a few days."

I hastened to explain that I figured on splitting our day's take with him, and that we could share the cost of food. I also told him it might take quite a while to clean up this particular spot I had in mind.

Happy took what meager belongings he felt he would need and climbed into the old Chevvy with me. We arrived back in camp to find that Dot had gone shopping again and had come up with three large steaks for dinner.

We installed Happy in the spare room in the cabin which we had been using for storage, and when supper was ready I thought his eyes would pop right out of his head.

Except for the steaks it was a very normal dinner, potatoes, a vegetable, homemade biscuits, a small green salad from our garden, and fresh berry cobbler for dessert. But to Happy, it was a banquet.

"I can't believe my eyes—you cooked this just for me," he said. "I've never had a meal that tasted this good!"

There is one thing I can say for that boy, he could sure eat. But, if Happy could eat, he could also work, his energy was boundless.

Next day Happy and I went down to where I had been working a long stretch of gravel-covered bedrock. By noon we had moved more yardage of gravel than I normally moved all day. In fact, I had to speed up the engine which powered the pump in order to get enough water into the sluice box to handle the larger volume of gravel we were moving into it.

At four o'clock that afternoon we shut down the pump and

cleaned up the sluice box. Happy took a look at the long trail of flakes and fine gold that washed from the sluice box into the gold pan and let out a yell of triumph.

"Look at that—why that's more gold than I've ever gotten in a week." Actually, when we weighed it on the gold scales as Dot was preparing supper, our day's take amounted to just a shade over six dollars. "Well, half of it is yours," I told him.

The success of our first day's joint venture spurred Happy on, and there was seldom a day we did not make five dollars or more, simply because of the amount of work he did. Happy became a permanent member of our family, and summer melted into fall.

September rolled around and one evening I drove up to see old Dan to suggest we think about cleaning up the remainder of the tailings at the rattlesnake mine. Dan agreed, but he was not feeling well, and suggested that Dot and I go to the mine without him.

"I'm old, and my miseries are bothering me. I think my mining days are about done," said the old man.

Nor was Dot overly enthusiastic about heading back for the mine and the possibility of more rattlesnakes. In fact, when it came down to a final decision, she was adamant in her determination not to go.

"You can go up there if you want to—take Happy with you—but I am not setting foot near that mine again. I've had all the rattlesnakes I need for a lifetime, and there isn't enough gold in that entire mountain to entice me back there again," Dot declared.

So, as a result of Dan's health and Dot's determination to have no part of the mine and its rattlesnake population, Happy and I piled mining equipment and grub into the Chevvy and early one morning set off for the mine.

The mine was exactly as we had left it. I don't think another human being had visited the area all summer, for there was neither wheel track nor footprint on the road or around the area of the mine itself. The cabins, except for their ever-present mouse and packrat population, lay undisturbed.

As we approached the meadow, again for about the fortieth time, I warned Happy about the rattlesnakes.

"Be careful—watch every place you step or put your hand—don't take a single chance, for there are rattlers everywhere," I warned him. We stopped the car, got out as if we were walking on eggs, and before each step we took, we looked carefully.

No rattlesnakes greeted us, and after the buildup I had given them, I think Happy was a little bit disappointed. In fact we opened up the cabin, cooked dinner and inspected the gravel tailings we were to begin mining the following morning, without seeing a single rattler.

Nor did we see a rattlesnake all the time we were at the mine. Before we finished, Happy was kidding me about the nonexistent snakes, and suggesting that I had just probably dreamed about them.

It took another full week's work to clean up the last of the mine tailings, and when we finished I estimated we had nearly five hundred dollars in raw gold. The last of the tailings had not been as rich as the first we had mined, but we still netted nearly seventy-five dollars a day. Happy was completely amazed. He had never before seen that much gold or any other kind of money at one time.

We returned to Downieville to find the country in a state of excitement. War had been declared in Europe, and everywhere there was speculation and rumor.

We sold the gold, and after dividing evenly with old Dan, who still was not really feeling well, Happy and I pocketed one hundred fifty-three dollars each. It was the most money, Happy said, that he had ever owned at one time. This would be a winter, he added, when he would have warm clothes and enough to eat.

There were unmistakable signs, also, that the Depression was drawing to a close. People were leaving the mountain counties for jobs in the shipyards. Lumbermills, virtually defunct during the Depression years, suddenly were hiring men. There still were snipers along the river, but not as many as there had been a year before, and somehow Dot and I could feel change coming—things were not the same.

Happy, who had been with us all summer, moved back into his own camp which he had set up about a half mile downstream from our cabin.

But a far different camp it was than the one we had found him living in a few months earlier. Happy had acquired a new tent and stove. He built a board floor on which to set the tent, much as we had done in our camp on the Agua Fria.

And now, with winter coming on, Happy had adequate food, warm clothes, and even more important, he had acquired confidence and a good, solid knowledge of sniping. He knew how to mine gold.

Happy left us, not because of any disagreement or dissatisfaction on either side. We still were good friends, and we saw him often. Happy moved to his own camp because he wanted to prove to himself that he could make a living on his own—that he could wrest a livelihood from this river with no one to depend on but himself. And this boy who until a couple of years ago had never been more than a stone's throw from the pavement of a large city—who had known nothing of the outdoors—suddenly had become a pretty good outdoorsman, and a better than average gold miner.

At least once a week Happy stopped by to have dinner with us and to exchange news of the latest goings on up and down the river. One evening just at dusk Happy arrived to inform us that he had gone into a mining partnership with a fellow who had arrived on the river only a few weeks earlier.

"He knows what this mining business is all about," Happy told us. "And he has a pretty good piece of ground he wants me to work with him. I think I'll give it a whirl because two men can accomplish so much more than one man working alone." I agreed with Happy and wished him luck. "But you know," I told him, "that if you want a partner you can work with me any time you want to."

A week went by and I saw nothing of Happy, and it was near the end of the second week before I saw him again.

I was chopping kindling one evening when Happy, carrying a knapsack loaded with supplies, strode down the trail on his way back from town.

"Pull that pack off and stay for supper," I told him. "We haven't seen you for so long I though you'd gotten lost." Naturally, in the progress of our conversation I asked Happy how the mining was going, and how his partner was working out.

Happy grinned. "Guess I forgot to mention it, but I'm back mining alone again. Joe was a real nice guy, honest, and he worked hard, too. But have you ever set up a sluice box and moved it three times in a single day because the spot you're working is pretty good, but the spot over there a few yards might be better?

"That's the way it went," said Happy. "We would just get going good—start getting some pretty good colors—and Joe would get the fidgets and grab a gold pan and begin prospecting someplace else. The minute he'd get a few colors at the new spot he'd be all hot to move the sluice box. Jess, you won't believe it, but we moved the damned sluice box three times in one morning.

"If I tried to talk him out of moving the rig to a new place, then Joe would get all pushed out of shape and pout the rest of the day. We spent more time moving than we did mining, and finally I told Joe that I thought the best thing for me would be to move back to my own diggings.

"The last thing I saw of Joe he was moving his sluice box across the river to a new spot he'd just found."

We had finished supper, lighted our cigarettes, and Dot was pouring second cups of coffee when Happy leaned back in his chair, took a deep drag from his hand-rolled smoke, and said:

"Guess there's one thing I haven't told you yet—I'm going to be leaving here pretty soon."

Dot set the hot coffeepot down in the middle of the oilcloth table cover and stood staring at the blond young man sitting across the table from us.

"Leaving? You mean you're leaving here—leaving the river—leaving Downieville and Sierra County? Where are you going, Happy? Why?"

Half embarrassed, Happy was looking down at the table.

"Well, I didn't tell anybody because I was afraid they'd think it was kind of silly. But the reason you didn't see me last week was because I went to Sacramento. Caught a ride on the mail truck to Nevada City, then took a bus on down there—and I went and joined the Army. I'll be leaving here next week."

Both Dot and I were caught almost speechless.

"Joined the Army—but why, Happy? We're not at war."

"Yes, I know," said the boy. "But we're going to be. They're already talking about preparedness, and about a draft. I figured I'd have to go sooner or later anyway, and if I go now—me who hasn't got anybody in this world, except maybe you two right here, maybe some other kid who has somebody at home won't have to go quite so soon."

Dot embarrassed the poor kid even worse by throwing her arms around him and kissing him. I didn't really know what to say except to wish him luck.

Meanwhile the hot coffeepot had burned a hole through the oilcloth table cover.

For months we had been reading in the paper and listening to the radio about the war in Europe, but it was that simple moment in our cabin on the Yuba River in tiny Sierra County that suddenly made the war a reality.

It was late that night before Happy left our cabin to walk down to his own lonely little camp on the river. Before he left we had completed arrangements to help move his camp and safely store all his belongings in Downieville.

For Dot and me the world had suddenly become a little more involved, and the war, far away in Europe, was suddenly much closer.

Three days later we watched the mail truck leave Downieville with Happy—its lone passenger—headed for Sacramento and the U. S. Army, and beyond that, no one knew what. Those of us who had turned out to say goodbye, including Tony, Judge Robbins, and a dozen or so other townspeople, stood watching the mail truck disappear down the road. There was a feeling of loneliness and personal loss among all of us.

To my knowledge it was the last time anyone of us who had known Happy, ever saw him again. We received an occasional letter from him for several months after his induction, and we know he was shipped out for duty in the Pacific. Happy's last letter arrived several months before December 7, 1941, and so far as I know, he did not return to Downieville after the war.

With Happy gone, Dot and I returned to work on the river, but hardly a week had passed when upon returning home from work one evening we found Roy and Ethel Topham at the cabin waiting for us.

Of course there were the usual greetings and excitement of having old friends with us again, but almost instantly I realized this was not totally a social greeting.

We had no more than gotten into the cabin out of the afternoon chill and had a fire going when Roy brought up the reason for his visit at this particular time.

"Well, Java, I hope you've had your fill of mining for gold, because whether you know it or not you're all through—you're going to work for Uncle Sam."

For several years Roy had been employed by the National Bureau of Standards as an inspector at a Santa Clara cement manufacturing plant. A similar job had opened up, and Roy had managed to work me into the position.

Although we had never planned to spend the remainder of our lives sniping for gold along the rivers of California, the offer took me completely by surprise. I looked at Dot and I was not sure whether she was about to laugh or cry. We finally managed to tell Roy and Ethel that I would take the job. A crazy thought kept running through my mind—I kept wondering how Ladybug would like it. All these years she had been free to roam the hills with us, and now she would find herself living in a city again, confined to an apartment and a small yard.

I was to report to work in two weeks and the following days became a nightmare of moving, travel, and of getting settled in a new place—of getting acquainted again with the hustle and bustle of city life.

We made two trips with the trailer to Ceres where we stored our mining equipment and camping gear with my dad. There were new clothes to buy, an apartment to find and become settled in, and it seemed there was never quite enough time to accomplish all the things that had to be done.

We had said hurried goodbyes to Tony Lavazolla and Judge Robbins; Downieville and the Yuba River country was behind us; and suddenly we were city residents again with an apartment in San Jose. It was a much different apartment and a much different world than the one we had existed in when we were first married.

The apartment was new, my new job paid well and I liked it. Within a few weeks we retired the poor, dilapidated old Chevvy and replaced it with a new car. Modern stores and shops were everywhere, with vast varieties of new clothing and merchandise. Yet there was a loneliness here, even though we were among friends, that neither Dot nor I had ever experienced in the mountains.

Ladybug was the most out-of-place and lonesome of all. She simply could not accustom herself to life in an apartment, broken once or twice a day by a short walk along paved streets or some busy parkway. She hated with a passion the leash we had to keep her on while walking her.

There were old friends to visit and many things to do on

my days off from work, yet we had been in the city only a few weeks when one morning on my day off, Dot suggested, as we were eating breakfast, that we visit the hills.

"Come on," she said, "let's get away from the city for a while. I want to smell the pine trees and see the wind blowing the grass again, and Ladybug just can't wait to get out and chase a squirrel." In twenty minutes a picnic lunch was packed and we were on our way out of town.

It was only a ride in the hills on a half-sunny not too warm winter day, but the fresh air never smelled so good. In a sheltered glade along a little foothill stream we stopped and ate our lunch. Ladybug ran free, the happiest little dog I have ever seen.

To leave those foothills that afternoon and return to San Jose was like forcing ourselves away from an old and cherished friend. The sights and sounds and smell of the mountain country lingered in our minds, and when, a few weeks later, a job as federal inspector at a cement plant in Calaveras County opened up, I jumped at the chance for transfer.

Within a month we were settled in a small home in San Andreas, a historic mining community in the brown, brush-covered foothills on Highway 49. We had seldom been to Calaveras County before, but it was like coming home.

Here at our doorstep was gold-mining country, and while this was a far cry from the metropolitan area of San Francisco, Oakland, and San Jose, it suited Dot and me and Ladybug real fine. For the first time in three months Ladybug seemed truly happy as she explored a vacant field near our new home.

The flag of Spain had flown over California soil for three centuries before that January day in 1848 when an itinerant carpenter at a place called Coloma, on the Rio de los Americanos, looked into a millrace and discovered flakes of gold.

And it was this chance discovery which triggered the greatest mass migration the western world has ever known.

Ultimately, it broke the back of resistance of the plains Indians, wrested half of the western U.S. from the threatening grasp of foreign powers, and, in the space of a decade, built a metropolis on a wilderness shore.

California gold helped build the first transcontinental railroad and contributed measurably to a Northern victory in the War between the States.

Nor is it surprising that a discovery of wealth in such quantity did so much to change history.

What is surprising is that history delayed this discovery for so long.

Like so many others, James Marshall, who made the historic discovery at John Sutter's mill on January 24, 1848, did not become rich from his find. Marshall died a poor and disillusioned man, but his lack of wealth was more a matter of bad luck than lack of gold in the streams and ledges of California's Mother Lode.

In 1852 more than $81,000,000 in raw gold was mined in California. Even in 1940, the last year of major gold-mine operation, that state's gold production was upward of $50,000,000. And a considerable share of the yellow metal mined during the 1930s and early '40s came from pan and sluice box of the snipers, jobless men and women driven by the Depression to the gold country along the western slopes of the Sierra.

Nor was it lack of gold that brought an end to gold mining as a major industry in the Golden State.

War and a once-again booming job market drew the snipers and prospectors from their gold camps back to the cities, and closed the larger mines to divert men and materials to the national defense effort.

Today, with price of gold in the U.S. still solidly pegged at $35 per ounce, as it has been since 1933, and with the cost of wages and materials more then quadrupled, large holders of gold properties choose not to reopen their mines.

But closure of the mines is a matter of economy rather than lack of gold.

Nor has the sniper of the 1930s returned to the gold country in force . . . job opportunities are too plentiful.

But the gold of the Mother Lode still is there. Along the rivers and creeks and in the white quartz ledges it lies, just as it did during Depression days and before.

Driven by necessity, as they were in 1930, men and women again could and would camp along the rivers and in the mountains, in tent or makeshift cabin, and earn their livelihood mining gold.

Mineralogists tell us that despite hundreds of millions of dollars in gold already taken, there still is more gold in the mountains of California than has ever been mined.

And constantly, their word is being proven true. The gold is here.

Reports of accidental gold strikes still are common. In Auburn parishioners cutting the foundation for a new church struck a ledge of gold ore. Only recently a quarry owner in Mariposa County, producing stone for building purposes, blasted by accident into a rich vein of gold.

Each weekend finds scores of gold prospectors, some with traditional pan and shovel, others with scuba gear, working along creeks and rivers in the gold country. And there are few whose efforts are not rewarded with at least a few yellow flakes or tiny nuggets as a result of an afternoon's work.

Then, scattered among the hills are still rugged individuals whose preference, even today, is to make their living mining gold.

It is not an easy life, but then, it was not easy in 1849 nor was it easy forty years ago.

But these men and women are proving to the world and to themselves that it can be done, that a living still can be made from gold.

And should worst ever come to worst again, there will be

many more who will join them, and they, too, will make their living once more, by mining gold.

Today our home in San Andreas is a far cry from the little canvas tenthouse on the Agua Fria, or the rustic cabin on the hill overlooking the Yuba River. I haven't shot a deer out of season in more than thirty years, and today we buy our fireplace wood by the cord instead of cutting it by the armful with ax and bucksaw. Yet there still are a few of us old-timers who snipe the creeks and rivers, and despite a century of miners who have been there ahead of us, we still come up with a bit of gold.

I may not work quite as hard today or for as long hours as I did as a young man on the Yuba River or on the Agua Fria, and Dot seldom accompanies me as she once did, but mining is my enjoyment and my relaxation. I've mined since I was a kid, and mining is in my blood. As long as I can lift a gold pan or still tramp these hills, I'll never quit mining.

A young woman stopped by to see us not long ago, and during the course of conversation, talk turned to the years when we sniped for gold in Sierra County and on the Agua Fria. Dot told of living in our little nine-by-twelve tenthouse, of carrying water from the spring, of warming ourselves by a campfire while we mined on rainy days, of gathering wild greens to supplement our diet of bacon and beans.

"I just don't see how you could stand it," commented our young visitor. Dot smiled, and there was a far-away look in her eyes. "You know," she said, "those were the best and the happiest days of our lives."